The Scars of Shame

by

Michael Limmer

*'My stronger guilt
defeats my strong intent.'*
Hamlet Act 3, Sc 3

This is a work of fiction.

The characters are products of the author's imagination,

and any resemblance to persons living or dead

is entirely coincidental.

The Scars of Shame

Copyright Michael Limmer 2024

Prologue: Normandy, 1944

He supposed he was alive. It didn't feel like it. His head ached abominably, and when he forced open his eyes he was blinded by acrid smoke. He heard gunfire: he was used to that after those past weeks. It sounded distant, however, fading away.

He tried to move, didn't know whether he could, because his body felt so numb. And there was the wetness too, the treacly stickiness on his hands, congealing on his rumpled tunic.

Slowly, his eyes became accustomed to the smoke, black and unforgiving. He could make out someone lying beside him, within touching distance.

At that moment, he couldn't recall what had happened. The world around him had exploded, collapsed into sudden darkness. That must account for why they were lying there.

He dabbed a hand against the crumpled form beside him. The hand came away wetter than before, stickier. He willed himself to roll over on to his side, a monstrous effort, come face to face with whoever his hunched-up companion might be.

Face to face. That was just it: a man, a being, who had no face. He had no idea who he'd been yet must have known him, maybe even talked to him. The corpse was unrecognisable.

Anonymous.

He couldn't feel shocked, for he remembered this was war. There'd been dead bodies on the beach when they'd landed. Some of them he must have known in life; some he'd joked and laughed with.

The pain thundering in his skull made him cry out feebly, left an idea there.

An idea, insidious as sin; more tempting than sin.

I need no longer be me. It would be better if I were no longer me.

He heard voices far off, listened carefully. They were speaking in English. Allies, friends. Even so, they must also be the enemy now.

As quickly as he was able, but not quickly, he found papers in a pocket of the corpse's ravaged tunic. His wet and bloody hand fumbled for his own papers, found and exchanged them clumsily.

No longer me. And who would ever know?

The voices were nearer now. He could discern the dim outline of figures through the haze. With every muscle straining, bursting, his head pounding, eyes gritty with smoke, he crawled away into the nearby undergrowth. It felt as if he'd travelled miles. As he looked back, the shadowy forms were vaguely visible.

"These two poor bastards over here have copped it."

"Better call for the meat wagon."

Voices without emotion. Eyes which had seen it all before. Voices and eyes reconciled to the sounds and sights of war.

He supposed he could have cried out. They would have heard him, and God knew he needed help, soaked in blood and racked with pain. But no: *no longer me.* He knew that way was best. He'd take his chance.

His senses had slowly returned, and he found himself on the edge of a forest. Eventually hauling himself to his feet, he stumbled through the trees and emerged on to a track.

Knowing it must lead somewhere, he blundered raggedly along it. For hours? For days? It seemed an endless journey; mindless too. But equally he believed it might be very little time at all.

He'd awoken to darkness. Finally, when he came out of the forest, day had dawned. The sun had risen behind distant hills, its bold rays blinding him. Over to his left, he saw buildings. A farm? It seemed miles away. Could it be real, or a mirage?

His head was swimming again, he was bleeding copiously, the pain becoming unbearable; and he staggered towards the sun, shielding his helpless eyes.

He felt himself falling; couldn't prevent it. He was suddenly crumpled on the ground, unable to move, his senses fading.

Then came a voice, anxious, shrill, and a shadow fell across him. His eyes stuttered open, as he heard a girl, speaking rapidly in French. Gentle hands cradled his throbbing head, and he gazed up, awestruck, into the face of an angel.

So, he was in heaven. A weary smile pinched his careworn face. He'd never expected to make it to there.

He heard her calling urgently for help. *"Maman! Papa! Ici un soldat anglais! Il est mal blessé!"*

He tried to answer her, to calm her down. No words came; for by then, he'd fainted far away.

Oxford, 1963

1

Neal Gallian awoke abruptly; awoke tense and anxious. That face again: he'd been edging towards a glimpse of it, the features blurred, threatening to become clearer with each step. But as he inched nearer, the figure withdrew into the shadow, and suddenly Neal was back where he knew, writhing on the ground, while Clyde sat slumped against the packing cases, not five yards away, his eyes staring sightlessly, accusingly, his uniform soaked in blood. One second earlier, quicker, braver, and Neal Gallian knew he might have saved him.

The dream wouldn't let him alone. It had been the best part of two years ago now. And once again, he'd dropped off in his armchair. He often did: the work in the fruit and vegetable warehouse had been physically taxing, the hours long and unforgiving. But that was by the by. The bottom line was that he was out of a job once more and wasn't too sorry. All the lugging around had started his shoulder up again. Old Barnett had assured him when he'd given him the job that he'd be dealing with the paperwork and 'a bit of lifting now and then'. But the minute he'd found out that Neal had been a copper, he'd started to pile on the lifting, then pretended to be sorry when he'd handed in his notice. So, Neal would be down at the Labour Exchange come Monday, looking for clerical work, and this time making sure it was just that.

He'd bumped into Tom Wrightson, his old station sergeant, only the other day. Tom had tried to talk him into re-joining the force, told him even DCI Pilling had been asking after him: *"We can't afford to lose coppers like Gallian, Tom."*

But Neal's heart wasn't in it, couldn't be. There were too many ghosts. He was desperate to exorcise them, but they simply wouldn't go away.

He got up, stretched and picked up his jacket. It was past opening time, and he'd nip down to the Farmers for a pint, maybe two. Not that he did a lot of drinking. He never had, not even after it had happened, and the temptation had been there. But he enjoyed the undemanding company at the

Farmers. Herbie Gunn, the landlord, had been grateful for his help when Friary Street had been on his beat a few years back, and the customers, mainly older men, were always sounding off about something. The current subject was the Great Train Robbery, which had taken place in August, a couple of weeks earlier.

There were about half-a-dozen of them now, crowded around the bar, nattering away. They greeted him with a nod, and Herbie bustled along to pull him a pint of Morrell's.

"Evening, Mr Gallian. Just the man."

Neal returned the greeting, not bothering to insist that Herbie used his Christian name. After all, old habits died hard.

"Bloke in here looking for you," the landlord went on. "Thought you might drop in, as it's Friday evening. He's over in the corner. Been here since we opened."

"What's he drinking?" Neal asked. If there was someone actually wanting to see him, it could be worth celebrating.

"Pint of mild and bitter, same as you."

Neal pitched a couple of coins on to the bar. "I'd better get him another, then."

Armed with the drinks, he made his way over to the corner, aware of a face looming up to greet him. The evening sun was pouring through the back window, so he couldn't make out the man's features. But he recognised the voice.

"Evening, Mr G. What's this, then? A peace offering?"

Jacko Manning? With his back to the window, Neal could see he'd guessed right. Manning was probably a bit older than him, late thirties, wiry build, dark hair in a widow's peak, lean, crafty face and merrily sparkling eyes. A likeable sort of bloke, whom you'd never trust too far.

"We'll call it that," Neal grunted, as he set down the glasses and shook the proffered hand.

"Well, thank you kindly, sir. Here's to your good health." Jacko raised his fresh pint, having already put away the first.

And talking of putting away...

Neal had sent Manning down for a short stretch some four years previously. Jacko had been driving the getaway car in a foiled bank raid, and Neal and Clyde Holt had given chase through winding streets and over some waste ground, which Jacko hadn't realised was a dead end.

Trapped, Jacko had ditched the car and tried to do a runner, but Neal had gone after him, brought him down with a flying tackle. Jacko hadn't put up a fight. "You collared me fair and square, guv'nor."

Neal and Clyde had taken him in; the only one they'd managed to catch. Manning quickly saw sense and named the others, got a few months shaved off his sentence. Before he went down, he asked to see Neal. "Decent bloke for a copper." Neal had given him some advice then. He asked him now if he'd taken it.

"You bet I have, since the day I went in. Even got time off for good behaviour. No, I've been repping these last couple of years – beers and spirits. This geezer in Brum took a chance on me, and I've never given him cause to regret it."

"Glad to hear it. So, what brings you back to Oxford? Is it your patch?" He'd noticed Jacko's suit: a bit creased, and his tie askew, as if he'd had a busy day.

"No, out Gloucestershire, Hereford way. Called here 'cos I felt I ought to see you." He hesitated, frowned. "Sorry to hear about your misfortune."

Neal shrugged, as if he was able to dismiss the memory so easily. "Comes with the job." He didn't need reminding that Clyde Holt hadn't got off so easily. "I appreciate your concern."

"Oh, it's a bit more than a social call." Jacko reached in a pocket and presented a dog-eared business card: *Bolsover Beers & Spirits: John W. Manning, Representative.* "Funny thing is, Oxfordshire's not my patch, but I was making some calls for another rep, who's off sick. And lo and behold, I ran into an old army pal. We got talking, and some information came my way that might interest you. It concerns your brother."

"Roger?" Neal wondered at the yelp of amazement in his response. Of course, Roger: he was the only brother he'd ever had.

Another ghost. Like the face he tried to recognise but could never see clearly. Like the dying Clyde. Like Helen…

He snapped out of it. "Sorry, Jacko. Carry on."

"Well, I'd been on the road for Bolsover the other night and missed the last bus back to Cheltenham, so I put up at this B & B in a place called Steenhampton off the main Cheltenham-Oxford road. I had time to kill, so went down to the local for a pint or three – a pub called the Chasing Hound. Swipe me, if I didn't run into Ted Stoker there, who I hadn't seen since the war. We were in North Africa together, see, before we got separate postings. Well, he was reg'lar down in the dumps and knocking it back like it had gone out of fashion. He downed five or six pints while I was with him. Blimey, I couldn't keep up with that – didn't even try. He went chuntering on 'bout his regrets – though we've all had a few of those – and he started up 'bout some incident in France after the D-Day invasion.

"He was getting maudlin to the point where I was dearly hoping he'd belt up and go home. Then he was saying how he wished he'd talked to his CO at the time. 'There was this chap Gallian,' he said. 'He couldn't speak up for himself, and I often wish I'd done it for him.'

"Well, Mr G, it never struck me till the middle of the night, when I woke up busting for a slash, that of course I knew a Gallian – your good self – and I recalled you'd told me something 'bout having lost a brother in the war."

Neal remembered there'd be one night in the cells when he'd been custody officer, and he and Jacko had got talking. He'd mentioned Roger then, how he'd gone missing during the war, and they'd heard nothing from or about him.

"I take it you've heard nothing since?" Jacko went on. Neal gave a peremptory shake of the head. "So, it might be worth your while getting in touch with Ted Stoker? Seems he's down at the Hound most nights."

Neal considered this, alert to Manning waiting eagerly on his reply.

"So, what would be in it for you, Jacko?"

He grinned laconically. "You know me too well, Mr G. I'll come out there with you, introduce you to Ted, like. And if anything comes of it, well, I shouldn't think you'd forget your old mate, would you?"

Neal doubted that the ex-con qualified as a mate, but he let it go. Jacko had come out of his way to do him what he saw as a favour. He told Jacko he had a date that evening and wondered if he'd mind postponing the trip to Steenhampton for twenty-four hours? The next day was Saturday, and Manning didn't mind staying overnight in Oxford, particularly when Neal offered to meet the cost of his B & B.

It seemed he might be expecting the meeting with Stoker to bear fruit. Neal wasn't so sure, not after all this time. He thought he'd better check up on some facts before plunging in.

2

Neal didn't have a date that evening; hadn't had one for some time. With everything that had happened, it had been a while since he'd given much thought as to what might have become of Roger. The passing of the years had distanced him from the brother he'd loved, and he decided he should fill in a few gaps in his memory before venturing out to Steenhampton with Manning.

Lionel Gallian, his father, had maintained contact with Roger's former CO. Lionel had always pretended otherwise, but right up until the day he'd died he'd held out hopes that Roger would return. So, when he got back to his flat that evening, Neal phoned Colonel Wilkie, who listened patiently before inviting him to call over the following afternoon.

Briar Hedge was the first of a few thatched cottages and bungalows scattered along a winding lane, three miles north-west of the Cotswold market town of Braxbury. As he drove on to the gravelled forecourt, to park alongside a mud-spattered and elderly Land Rover, the sight of the once-white walls gushing with climbing roses stirred a memory of the one occasion when he'd called before.

The crunch caused by his old Consul's tyres heralded his arrival, and within seconds, a girl appeared through a wicket gate to the side of the cottage. She set down the trug she'd been carrying, peeled off her gardening gloves and approached with a welcoming smile, as he emerged from the car.

He put her in her early twenties, her face pretty if a little pale, fair hair tied back in a ponytail. Blue eyes appraised him cautiously from behind pink-framed spectacles. She was slightly built, trim in blue check blouse and black slacks.

"Mr Gallian?" She thrust out a hand which he shook, fragile in his ham-like grasp. "I'm Jill Westmacott. Uncle Lam asked me to look out for you. He's in the summerhouse round the back, if you'd like to follow me?"

She led him through the wicket gate and across a back lawn bordered by shrubs. The garden looked in good order, and Neal guessed that might be down to her efforts.

His first sight of the summerhouse confirmed it. The flat-roofed wooden shack had seen better days. The roses scaling the walls and wriggling across the roof probably played their part in preventing the collapse of the building.

Jill pushed her head and shoulders through the open doorway. "Mr Gallian's here, Uncle Lam," she announced and, turning to Neal, added, "I'll bring you some tea."

"Thank you. That'd be very kind." They exchanged shy smiles, and the girl crossed the lawn and entered the cottage through some open French windows. Neal stepped into the summerhouse.

The September sunshine poured through a skylight to illuminate the interior. The desk was blanketed with piles of papers, which seemed in no particular order, and a man rose from behind it. He reached across, offering a hand, and Neal moved forward to shake it.

"Lambert Wilkie, Mr Gallian. I remember your name well. Do take a seat, if you can find one. Jill steadfastly refuses to tidy up in here. But it's my hideaway, second home if you like, and, as you can see, replete with memories."

Neal found himself liking Wilkie right away. He'd recently retired from the army with the rank of colonel, a short, stocky man in the late fifties, with a grizzled face, and hair and eyebrows of a forbidding grey.

He was right about the den: a real glory-hole with army mementoes everywhere. Rows of medals and portraits of every stage of Wilkie in uniform lined the walls, while behind the desk hung a large framed photograph of the company he'd commanded. Neal guessed it dated from the war and supposed that Roger might be in it, but he didn't want to ask about it or take a closer look.

"Uncle Lam's writing his memoirs." The girl appeared in the doorway bearing a tea tray, and Wilkie scrabbled around at the desk to make room for it. "And sadly, they're taking over." But she spoke with affection and was looking on in amusement.

"Jill despairs of me," Wilkie sighed. "Her parents run a school in Nairobi, and she must be counting the days until she goes out and joins them."

"Nonsense," Jill replied. "You're not so bad, Uncle Lam, and it's not definite I shall go anyway." She poured the tea and handed a cup to Neal, then to her uncle. Again, the shy smile, as she took her leave. "I'll be working on the borders," she told them. "Just call out if you want more tea."

She crossed the lawn, retrieved her trug and could soon be heard clipping vigorously away with her secateurs. Colonel Wilkie nodded after her fondly.

"Grand little girl," he said. "My sister's daughter, and a chip off the old block." He reached in a drawer, fetched out a tobacco tin and started to fill a pipe which he retrieved from among his papers. "Well, Mr Gallian. Tell me what brings you here?"

Neal was pretty sure he'd already guessed but explained anyway.

"An -er, old acquaintance of mine came to me last night with a story, Colonel, and I wanted to verify a few facts with you. You see, it concerns my brother."

Wilkie nodded briskly, as he put a match to the bowl of his pipe. "Roger. Yes, I wondered if it might."

"This acquaintance had run into an old army colleague at a pub called the Chasing Hound at Steenhampton."

"I know it – five or six miles east of here."

"The colleague's name is Ted Stoker. He said he had information relating to Roger."

Wilkie frowned as he began drawing on his pipe. "What kind of information?"

"I don't know as yet. I'm meeting him at the pub this evening to find out. If Stoker knew Roger, I assume he was in your company in France?"

"That's right, he was. Joined in late '43, as I recall. He'd served in North Africa." He jabbed the stem of his pipe in Neal's direction. "I have to say, that if I'd been in a position to hand-pick my men, Private Stoker wouldn't have been among them. Rather shady, I seem to remember. Also, if he has any worthwhile information, why hasn't he come forward at any time during the last nineteen years? Why wait until now? I'd recommend, Mr Gallian, that you take anything he says with a generous pinch of salt."

Neal grinned tightly. "I should anyway. Ten years with the police taught me that."

"Oh? You're a policeman?"

His grin became rueful. "Not any longer."

Wilkie's brusque nod implied that he understood. Neal felt he'd recognised the note of dejection in his reply. But in any case, the colonel didn't pursue the matter.

The ensuing silence might have proved awkward, but Neal hadn't yet got what he'd really come for. He was under no illusion about Stoker, but his curiosity had been aroused, his sense of duty too.

"I'd like you to tell me exactly what happened, Colonel. My father only told me so much. And he's no longer around to expand on that."

"Oh? I'm sorry to hear that."

"Thank you. No, what he learned from you he kept for the most part to himself."

He recalled that afternoon, Lionel Gallian emerging from the cottage where he'd been closeted with Lambert Wilkie. He looked sterner than ever, and the young Neal, heart hammering fitfully, looked up imploringly at his father, dreading to hear anything bad about the elder brother he'd revered.

"Is Roger dead, Father?" The words leaked out in a choked whisper.

Lionel Gallian couldn't meet his gaze. "He's dead to me," came his glum reply.

3

"We came here at the end of the war, didn't we?" Neal went on. "Soon after VE Day. It was a summer's afternoon. You took Father indoors, and I stayed out on a seat in the garden. A lady brought me a glass of lemonade and some cake."

Lambert Wilkie smiled indulgently. "That was my sister Janet, Jill's mother. She took me to task for abandoning you without having offered any refreshment. *'That poor boy looks so unhappy.'*"

Neal allowed himself a brief smile. He could still recall the delicious tang of the home-made lemonade, the sweet crunch of the rock buns. The lady's kindness had partly alleviated his gloom.

"Your father took the news hard," Wilkie said.

"He loved Roger dearly. Saw him as an officer in his own image. As soon as war was declared, Roger abandoned his university course and enlisted. Father had fought with distinction in the Great War and visualised Roger emulating him. After Roger -er, went away, Father was never the same man. He started to go steadily downhill from that moment. He passed away three years ago."

Lionel Gallian had been a strict parent, yet seldom unfair. He'd come to terms with Neal joining the police after his spell of National Service had persuaded him that an army career was not for him. Indeed, going by Neal's earlier memories, Lionel might be said to have mellowed. But in truth he'd given up: a sad, proud, dour man slowly relinquishing his grip on life, because it ceased to hold anything for him. Although Neal was sure his father would have reacted spiritedly against his decision to quit the police.

Wilkie jabbed the pipe in Neal's direction again, his face partly hidden behind a plume of smoke. He imagined the fug inside the shack with the door closed would have much in common with the notorious London smog. It was small wonder Jill Westmacott wouldn't clean in there.

"I remember you," the colonel exclaimed. "Janet, my sister, was full of praise. *'Such a polite boy, and so brave. He seemed a bit bewildered by it all, although that's hardly surprising.'*"

"I *was* bewildered," Neal admitted. "I adored Roger and simply couldn't understand why he'd done that." He pictured his brother: dark hair and eyes, olive-skinned, rarely unsmiling and to him never less than kind.

"He was much older than me," he went on. "By almost nine years. I couldn't understand why he didn't return when the war ended. I suppose Father must have been too ashamed to go into detail. Mother had been in poor health for some years, and in his opinion, I was too young to understand, so he tried to spare us the truth. I believe he convinced Mother that Roger was dead, but his knowledge slowly destroyed him. Some time before he died, he told me that Roger had deserted and been court-martialled in his absence. There was something about a chateau and a reconnaissance party. They came up against opposition, and, inexplicably, Roger ran away."

Colonel Wilkie looked pained as he settled back in his chair. "I was Roger's CO for the duration of the D-Day invasion and its aftermath," he said. "It happened soon after we'd occupied the town of Valleronde. Just outside it lay the Chateau Garay, which Jerry had used as an HQ. It had belonged to a Jewish banker and his wife, who were taken away and never seen again. The place was stuffed with various paintings and other *objets d'art.* We had information that the local commandant had been a museum curator before the war, and it was feared he might have made off with as much as he could carry. Our brief was to secure what we could, so that in time it might be restored to the legal owners or, failing that, be auctioned off to replenish some of the museums and galleries Jerry had looted. The local resistance assured us Jerry had cleared out, but even so when I detailed Lieutenant Gallian to go up there, I warned him to watch his step, as the enemy wasn't above leaving one or two snipers around to make our lives uncomfortable.

"They went up at dusk: Roger, Bill Crannock his sergeant, two privates and a resistance man who guided them up through the woods to enable them to skirt round to the rear of the chateau. One of the privates was your man Stoker. That's why I'd be surprised if he knew anything beyond the official version which I'm giving you now.

"We were right about the snipers. The other private, a soldier named Doyle, got hit. Fortunately, it was only a flesh wound, and the man was determined to carry on. But he was losing a lot of blood, and Lieutenant Gallian ordered him back to base to get it seen to. Sergeant Crannock later told me that he and Roger worked out the snipers' positions: there were two of them. They plugged one, and the other turned tail and ran, although Crannock thought he might have winged him.

"Lieutenant Gallian went after him. Crannock said he was surprised at that, for he didn't see the need. Before he went, Roger ordered Crannock and the rest to check out the chateau. They did so and hung around for a while afterwards, pending further orders. But Roger never came back.

"On Sergeant Crannock's suggestion, they searched the grounds. It was possible that Roger had been ambushed and wounded, but they'd heard no shots and found no sign of anything untoward having happened. And of course, Roger never returned to base."

Colonel Wilkie ended on what was almost a note of apology, and it took a few seconds for Neal to realise he'd finished speaking. He'd listened spellbound to Wilkie's tale, for he'd been hearing parts of it for the very first time. One thing his father had mentioned, was that he'd gathered from Roger's last letter home that his son hadn't been well. Neal said as much to the colonel.

Wilkie knocked out the remains of his pipe into an ashtray and frowned at it studiously. "Roger worried me," he said finally. "He was one of my brightest young officers, but like the rest of them, he was under immense pressure. The D-Day landings had been no picnic, and the prospect of the invasion had been hanging over the men for months, for none of us had been given an inkling as to when it might take place. I believe he lost his best friend on Gold Beach, and that affected him deeply, may even have played a part in unnerving him."

Neal nodded his understanding. He recalled the friend, Philip Norreys, also the son of a military man. He and Roger had become fast friends at boarding school, both keen rugby players and cricketers. Philip had often stayed for part of the holidays, and at other times Roger had gone to stay with him. The boys had been as close as brothers, and Neal recalled the thrill of being allowed to tag along with them on their country rambles – 'adventures', he'd called them – and playing cricket and even going sailing with them.

Colonel Wilkie sighed. "It was a long and wearying campaign, Mr Gallian. I saw Roger as a gentle soul, and he was hit hard by his friend's death. It seems he simply lost his nerve and bolted. It's often a minor incident which can trigger that. Believe me, I've known it happen.

"Once Sergeant Crannock had reported back, I ordered a full-scale search of the chateau's grounds and the surrounding area, but all we found was the body of the first sniper. It seemed likely that Crannock had indeed winged the other man, for we discovered a trail of blood but no body. And there was no sign of Roger.

"I questioned the men from the reconnaissance party again, but neither Stoker nor the resistance chap, whose name I forget, could add anything. Only Sergeant Crannock had witnessed Roger dashing off after the second sniper."

Wilkie spread his hands in apology. "I'm sorry, Mr Gallian. I liked your brother. He was intelligent, a good officer and respected by his men. Bill Crannock and I spoke up for him at the court martial, but to no avail. Something must have snapped that day, and he took off. He could have made his way down to Spain, may even still be in France. I assure you we did all we could at the time, although our resources were limited, and we were under orders to push on almost immediately."

"Then you believe that he actually deserted?" Neal couldn't hide his disappointment. "That he simply ran away?"

"Let me be frank. I'm unable to see it any other way. My first reaction was one of shock, and it's something I've often puzzled over. Because it was so unlike him, and I'd known him quite a while, believe I've enough experience to get the measure of a man. However, we each have our tipping point." Wilkie leaned back in his chair, steepled his fingers and regarded Neal steadily.

For his part, Neal was struggling to hang in. He'd called on Wilkie first, because there were parts of the story his father had never shared with him. The colonel had duly filled in those gaps, and Neal felt he was heading towards a brick wall. He couldn't see what Ted Stoker might possibly add, because it all appeared cut and dried, with no room for doubt. He found himself clinging desperately to a recollection from his childhood, an incident from a few years before the war.

He must have been five or six years old, and Roger in his early teens. They'd been out for a ramble, and he'd been dawdling across a field, fifty yards behind his brother. There'd been horses in the field, and Neal had had to pass them to reach the stile. The horses had followed and, frightened, he'd started to run. They'd charged after him, and he'd tripped and fallen. Roger, alert to the danger, had sprinted back and snatched him out of the horses' path. It had been an act of great bravery and love, and it had summed up Roger. Neal had revered him: surely, he could never have *run away*? And yet for years he'd accepted it, caught up in his father's gloom and apathy.

But for now, he held fast to that memory, as he asked, "What about the man who was wounded? Might he know anything?"

Colonel Wilkie was too polite to tell him he was snatching at straws. "Private Doyle." He shook his head. "I'm afraid he was back at base by the time it all happened. His wound still hadn't healed a couple of days later, when my company was ordered to move on. Doyle followed on a week or so afterwards with another company. Sadly, they ran into trouble, and Doyle, along with several others, was killed."

Again, the brick wall. Neal supposed he might have known that. He got to his feet and thanked Wilkie for his help. As they shook hands, he apologised for having taken up so much of the colonel's time.

"Not at all," he replied kindly. "It's right that you should know all the details. But my advice is not to believe too readily anything friend Stoker may tell you."

Neal smiled. "I won't."

"And do get back in touch if there's anything more I can do."

Neal thanked him again and went out into the garden, where Jill Westmacott was snipping energetically away at a laurel bush. She looked up as he appeared, and her face clouded as she saw his dismay.

"Is everything all right, Mr Gallian?" She set down her secateurs and, with a wave at her uncle who stood in the doorway of the summerhouse, accompanied Neal round to his car.

"Not really," he replied. "Your uncle's been most helpful but, well, I'm not sure where I go from here – if anywhere."

She nodded sympathetically, but he didn't feel like going over the whole story again. Neither did he wish to envelop her in his personal gloom, so he changed tack, asking if she worked locally?

She smiled. "Apart from skivvying for Uncle Lam, you mean? Yes, I help out in Mr Vernon's wine shop in Braxbury High Street. I get on very well with his wife." She glanced over her shoulder before lowering her voice. "My parents run a school in Nairobi and keep pestering me to go out and join them. But I've got used to being here and really don't know how Uncle Lam would fare alone."

They reached his car and, as they shook hands, Jill expressed the wish that everything would work out for him. In spite of himself, Neal felt lifted by that and thanked her. But as he drove away, he began to feel low again. Jacko Manning's tale had brought him brief respite, for he'd hoped he might learn something about what had happened to Roger.

He decided to keep the rendezvous with Ted Stoker that evening, for it was the only way to find out if his information was reliable. Although after what Wilkie had told him, he doubted that he'd learn anything new.

4

Just after eight o'clock, he picked up Manning from the corner of St Margaret's Road and headed west out of Oxford along the A40. Jacko seemed to cut a slightly despondent figure, although Neal didn't remark upon it, as the mood coincided with his own. He wondered if perhaps Manning also had doubts that the meeting with Stoker was likely to bear any fruit.

As they turned off the A40 to dip down into the valley of the Windrush, with the river gleaming in the late evening sun and the surrounding fields a patchwork of green, brown and gold, Jacko finally stirred himself. Conversation had been spasmodic at best, and Neal had waited patiently to learn his companion's opinion on the matter.

"Just been thinking, Mr G. See, Ted Stoker's a suspicious sort of cove, and he'd probably reckon I'm out to get myself a piece of the action. I guess it'd be best if I pointed him out to you and waited outside, if you don't object. Else he might clam up."

Neal took his point and agreed to go along with it. But it confirmed his suspicion that Jacko thought Stoker would have little or nothing to contribute. However, as they were at that moment driving into the village of Steenhampton, there seemed no point in turning back.

Jacko suggested they park in a side street and continue to the pub on foot. The pub's car park was likely to be full, as this was a Saturday night. Neal did so, and they walked through the narrow streets to the Chasing Hound.

It stood on the far edge of the village, a rambling coaching inn in yellowing brick, set back from the road. Jacko had been right: the gravelled area to the side and rear of the pub was replete with cars, vans and motorbikes.

Manning walked across to a window and peered in. Standing at his shoulder, Neal could see that the pub was busy. There was a darts match going on, which was generating a lot of noise.

"That's him. That's Ted." Jacko jabbed a finger towards a figure slumped on a bar stool just beyond the window, a pint glass at his elbow. The darts match was in progress on the far side of the horseshoe-shaped bar, and while other spectators occupied a number of stools, Neal felt there was something solitary and disconsolate about the man Jacko had indicated.

"Okay. Wait here," Neal said, although Manning had already begun to melt back into the lengthening shadows.

"Best of luck, Mr G," he murmured, as Neal headed towards the pub's side door. Neal wished he might have heard some conviction in those words.

He went in. The darts match was well under way, and the other side of the bar packed with players and spectators. A small group along to Neal's left were watching avidly, but Ted Stoker didn't seem to show much interest, as he sat looking glum with a dwindling pint at his elbow.

Neal approached him. "Excuse me. Ted Stoker?"

The man looked up. He was large and untidy with greasy dark hair in need of a trim, and dull, wary eyes. "Who wants to know?"

"We've got a mutual friend. Jacko Manning."

"Who? Oh, right. Of course – old Jacko." Stoker laughed, more of a hacking cough than an expression of mirth. He knocked back the rest of his pint and slammed down the empty tankard. "So, mister. What about it?"

Neal took the unsubtle hint and signalled the barman, who pulled Stoker a fresh pint. Neal asked for a half of mild, paid the man and waited until he'd moved away.

He turned back to Stoker, who was taking a greedy slurp of beer. "Jacko reckoned you might have some information concerning my brother?"

A raucous cheer went up from around the dart board, and Stoker's attention was suddenly diverted there. "Oh, right. Who's that, then?" he asked distractedly.

Neal was having to shout to make himself heard. "His name's Roger Gallian. It's about something which happened in France – Valleronde, in Normandy, 1944."

As luck would have it, the cheering subsided halfway through his sentence, so that the whole pub heard him, and Neal happened to catch the keen gaze of a man across the bar. He guessed he was one of the darts players, but he'd moved back from the board to chat with a short, plump individual in shirtsleeves and a green felt hat, who was leaning back against the bar.

The man, tall with close-cropped hair, wore a crisp, white polo shirt and jeans. He was in middle age, lean and muscular. There was an air of authority about him, and Neal guessed anyone would think twice before picking a quarrel with him. He held Neal's gaze for a few seconds, a hard, appraising stare, before turning to respond to something the man in the hat had said. Seconds later, he re-joined the group around the dart board.

Stoker had clocked the man too. He'd kept his gaze averted, drinking deeply from his tankard. Now he flashed Neal a nervous glance.

Neal pitched his voice lower. "Jacko said you were talking about it the other night, that you felt you ought to have seen your CO at the time. It was something that happened at the Chateau Garay, in the town of Valleronde which your company had just liberated. Listen, if you've got information I can act upon, I'll pay for it. All I want is to be able to trace my brother." As he spoke, he was aware of the mounting desperation in his own voice; or maybe it was already despair.

Ted Stoker didn't reply. He swallowed the remains of his beer and blundered down off the stool. Neal shifted across and blocked his path to the door.

"What's your problem?" he asked reasonably.

Stoker cast an apprehensive glance across the bar, but the tall man was in the thick of the darts match, the noise level high again, and his friend in the green felt hat intent on watching, his back to the bar.

"Listen, mister," Stoker gabbled. "I can't talk now. Tell Jacko the situation's changed. Him and me, we had a few jars, see; hadn't seen one another since the war. We talked and talked, see, and p'raps I said too much, p'raps he misunderstood what I was saying, but he had no right to pass it on. I made a mistake, okay? All I know is that what they say happened to the lieutenant, well, that's the way it happened. Listen, I really got to go now. So long."

Nimbly for such an ungainly man, Ted Stoker squeezed past Neal and out through the door. Darkness had fallen, and Neal, following Stoker out, watched as he lumbered off into the gloom, gravel squirting from under his heavy feet.

As Neal let the door swing shut behind him, Jacko Manning materialised from the shadows. He nodded after the now invisible Stoker.

"In a heck of a rush, ain't he? What did he have to say?"

"He won't talk," Neal replied flatly. "Says it was all a mistake." He jerked a thumb towards the pub. "If you ask me, somebody in there spooked him."

"I can go after him, if you like, Mr G," Jacko offered. "See if I can talk him round?"

Neal shook his head. "Forget him for now. Instead, I'd like you to take a look at a bloke in the pub and tell me if you recognise him."

He turned towards the window, and Jacko, who'd been expecting to go off to reclaim Stoker and was several yards away, shrugged shoulders and started to follow.

Neal heard it first; the roar of an engine, scrunch of rapid tyres. The dark shape of a van burst out from behind the pub and headed straight for them. Yelling a warning, Neal leapt for the doorway, heard Jacko's cry as the van sped past them and away.

He hurried over to where Manning had fallen. He'd been lucky to scramble out of the way in time, and Neal helped him to his feet.

"Whew!" Jacko gasped. "That was a close call. Thought it was all up with me there. Ruddy idiot!"

"Did you see anything?"

Jacko shrugged peevishly. "What was there to see? A van with no lights, driven by a moron. No, Mr G. Not a hope."

"Me neither."

"Huh. Call yourself a copper?"

Jacko was close enough to see that his feeble attempt at levity hadn't been well received.

"Sorry, Mr G," he apologised. "Nerves are a bit shot after that little escapade. Mind if we wander back to the car and head off?"

"Sounds like a good idea." Neal clapped him on the shoulder. "I guess somebody around here doesn't like us."

Jacko held his gaze, his face deadly serious. "And I'd say you'd be right, pal. One hundred per cent right."

5

They crossed the road from the car park, Manning leading at a brisk pace. Neal reckoned the incident must have unnerved him more than he'd care to admit.

The street was dark and narrow, the only lighting a glow behind the occasional windowpane. The houses crowded along both sides of the street, tall and grim in the darkness, appearing to tilt towards them, almost forming a canopy.

To Neal, it seemed a long way back to his car. They'd left it in a side street but hadn't come across a turning as yet. Jacko seemed to be in no doubt, however, as he strode on ahead.

Suddenly the noise of an engine drowned the slight echo of their footsteps. Half-turning, Neal was blinded by the silent scream of headlights. He flung up an arm to shield his eyes, then, realising the vehicle was almost upon him, stumbled into the shelter of a doorway.

He had a brief glimpse of a short, squat van as it blasted past: a Commer or Morris, he guessed. He yelled a warning for Jacko, saw through the gloom the silhouette of a running man fleeing in the glare of lights which illuminated the whole street.

As the winking taillights disappeared around the next bend, he hurried along, wondering if Jacko had been hit. But he'd heard no cry and shortly came upon a narrow alley between two cottages. From somewhere along it, he made out the sound of rapidly departing footsteps.

Neal hurried on towards his car, realising that the side street where he'd parked was beyond the bend. Before he could reach it, the street was lit up again.

His first thought was that the van driver was returning for another attempt. He noticed with horror that there was now no pavement and, as the headlights came on, he flattened himself, arms spread-eagled, against the wall of a house.

The vehicle slowed down, and it occurred to him that it hadn't been going that fast in the first place. As the window wound down, a voice he'd heard before said with some concern, "Is something the matter, Mr Gallian?"

It was Jill Westmacott, and Neal recognised the Land Rover she was driving as her uncle's.

"Er, well…" He felt all kinds of a fool, backed up against a wall with no-one else in sight. And he couldn't make excuses: something was definitely the matter, as she would have seen from his startled expression.

"Er, a bit of trouble," he went on. "I think we may have upset someone. A van was just driven down the street at us at some speed."

"Us?" Her gaze raked the darkness.

"My -er, pal. He ran off."

She smiled tightly. "Hop in. We'll drive around and look for him."

"Thanks. That's really good of you." It made sense too, because she obviously knew the village, and he didn't. He walked round and climbed into the passenger seat.

Jill put the Land Rover into gear. "Didn't you ought to phone the police?" she asked, as they set off. "About the van, I mean?"

He shook his head. "It happened too quickly for me to get the number or a glimpse of the driver." But he was sure it had been a Commer or Morris van. He'd remember that and stay alert.

She drove slowly around the village, but he saw no sign of Jacko Manning. Finally, he asked her if she'd take him back to his car and thanked her for her trouble.

"No trouble at all. I was on my way back from choir practice at Ashton Leigh, the next village along the valley." She hesitated. "Mr Gallian, I'm sorry – I don't mean to pry..."

"Please – it's Neal."

She smiled. "And I'm Jill." Her face grew serious again. "Tonight – the van. Is it connected with what you came to see Uncle Lam about this afternoon?"

He wondered how much she might have heard, not that he suspected her of eavesdropping. But if he was going to trust Wilkie – and he was certain he would, because he felt he might need an ally – why shouldn't he trust Wilkie's niece too?

"The man we were looking for just now," he said. "Jacko Manning. He's an old acquaintance. Let's say I -er, knew him when I was with the police."

"Arrested him, you mean?" She was certainly on the ball.

"Right. Likeable sort of bloke, for a villain. Although, according to him, he's going straight now. He came to see me yesterday, told me he had information from a man named Ted Stoker about my brother Roger, who went missing during the war." He took a deep breath and told her about Roger, his desertion from the reconnaissance party at Chateau Garay.

Telling it brought the old pain back, and he supposed it was because he'd kept it suppressed for so long; not given it much thought with all the bitterness over Clyde's death, over Helen's departure. And before that, there'd been his father: Lionel, sinking into illness and depression, unable at times to bear the mention of the name of that son who'd once been so dear to him.

Jill listened sympathetically, as if she sensed his inner turmoil. He tried not to sound too despondent.

"I came to see your uncle yesterday, because there were certain gaps in my knowledge. I also wanted to ask if he knew Ted Stoker. He did: he was Stoker's CO in Normandy. He also told me he didn't think the man particularly trustworthy. Having met Stoker, I'm inclined to agree. Stoker ran away – hadn't meant to say what he'd said to Jacko, reckoned it was all a big mistake, and to forget it."

"And will you?"

In the feeble light from the dashboard, her eyes seemed to glint behind their lenses. He perceived it as a challenge, but his answer was ready anyway.

"No. Not now."

"Do you think it might have been Stoker driving the van?"

It was an idea, but Neal shook his head. "I doubt it. But I intend to find out who was."

He opened the passenger door, feeling he'd taken up too much of her time. She forestalled him. "Er, Neal?" He turned back. "Do you mind if I mention this to Uncle Lam? There may be some way he can help."

"Please feel free. And thanks again for the lift."

"I hope your – friend – hope he's okay."

"Me too. Goodnight – Jill."

He watched her drive away, then got back in his own car and drove slowly back through the village and up to the main road, keeping an eye open for Manning all the way. He saw no sign of him.

By the time he'd reached Oxford and parked, it was gone eleven. Neal locked the car and made his way back to his digs. The house was in darkness, although this was unsurprising, as Mrs Pendle, his landlady, tended to retire early. She slept at the back of the terraced house, while Neal occupied the larger upstairs room. He'd been granted use of the kitchen "at a reasonable hour", although more often than not he cooked on the two-ring Belling in his room. He'd moved there once he'd come out of hospital. The flat in Headington had had too many associations, and the narrow South

Oxford street, lined either side with small, elderly red-brick terraces, suited his need for quietness and anonymity.

He hadn't been back long, sitting fretting over a cup of cocoa and hoping Manning hadn't come to any harm, when he heard a noise downstairs. He went to the door and eased it open, leaned out on to the landing and listened. The noise seemed to have come from the back of the house, highly likely the kitchen.

Neal squeezed out on to the landing and stole downstairs in his stockinged feet. Fortunately, Mrs Pendle was snoring away volubly, and from past experience he doubted she'd awaken for some time.

He felt a draught whistling under the kitchen door, as he padded towards it. Either the back door hadn't been fastened properly, or a window left open. He turned the knob and gently pushed open the door.

Neal was able to tell right away that the dark shape crouched apologetically beside the sink was Jacko Manning, and his first emotion was one of relief.

"Good to see you, Jacko," he whispered. "I was beginning to wonder."

Jacko unfurled himself to his full height, which wasn't much, and Neal caught the ghost of a grin. "Ought to get that kitchen window properly fixed, Mr G," he whispered back. "Never know what might happen with all these villains around."

Neal went over and fastened it. "Better come up to my room," he said. "And quietly. My landlady wakes up and finds you here, we're both in the soup."

He led Jacko upstairs, sat him down and made more cocoa, offering the two rich tea he had left in the biscuit tin. Jacko fished them out gratefully and ate them, his movements abrupt and jerky. When he spoke, his voice held no trace of his usual bravado.

"Whoever was in that van meant business. I managed to dodge him, get up to the main road and hitch a lift. I was glad to get away from there in one piece."

Neal asked the question Jill had raised earlier. "Jacko, I take it there's no way it might have been Stoker driving that van?"

"Ted?" Manning's tone was contemptuous. "Not the way he shot off from the pub. Faster than ruddy Robbie Brightwell. And that van was waiting round the back, I don't care what anyone says." He paused, flashed Neal a desperate glance. "It was me he was after all right, Mr G. Reckon somebody must've overheard me and Stoker talking the other night. You ask me, I'd say there's something in this after all."

Neal nodded his agreement as he took this in. His thoughts returned to the darts player in the Chasing Hound, and he described him to Manning. "Any idea who he might be?"

Jacko shook his head. "Don't know him. But from what you say, he must be the one who spooked Ted, and someone who lives locally into the bargain."

Neal followed up with a description of the man in the green felt hat, who'd been leaning back against the bar in conversation with the darts player. But Jacko was certain he didn't know him either. He turned to Neal pleadingly.

"Listen, Mr G. I don't mind telling you this has put the wind up me good and proper. I reckon I ought to lie low for a few days. I've got some time owing, so I'll phone my guv'nor in the morning, if you're okay with this. Tell him I got a sick relative to visit, who's at death's door."

"Better phone your wife too," Neal suggested. "Won't she be worrying?"

A trace of the old chirpiness resurfaced in Jacko's manner. "Stroll on, Mr G. What would I want with one of them? Footloose and fancy free, that's me."

"Fine. Have you got somewhere to hang out?"

"How about here?"

Neal imagined that an unexpected guest would put Mrs Pendle in a real lather. He thought the darts player might have clocked him too, and it wouldn't be too difficult to find out where he lived.

"I don't think so," he replied. "But don't worry. I think I know where I might be able to put you up for a few days, and it's some distance from here. You can have the sofa for tonight, and we'll get moving early in the morning."

6

They set off before Mrs Pendle had stirred. Neal left a note on the kitchen table to say he'd be back some time during the afternoon, confident that she'd assume he'd taken himself off for a hike, as he often did at weekends.

He made Manning wait in the hallway while he checked the street. The van driver had clearly been no fan of Jacko, and Neal didn't want to take any unnecessary risks.

However, the street was deserted, as might have been expected at that hour. They stopped off in Jericho, and Neal went into the B & B to retrieve Jacko's battered suitcase, leaving his companion in the car. He apologised for Mr Manning's non-appearance the previous night: he'd met with a minor accident, nothing serious, and Neal had just collected him from the Radcliffe Infirmary. The landlady clucked sympathetically but still allowed Neal to fork out for the room: two nights rather than one.

Back in the car, they headed out of the city through Botley and picked up the A420 towards Swindon. Neal knew the A40 would have been a more direct route to his intended destination, but he didn't want to go anywhere near Steenhampton, in case the van driver was out and about and happened to spot them.

After a few miles, he was sure there wasn't any pursuit, turned off at Faringdon, and beyond Lechlade picked up a series of country lanes which eventually got them to the quiet Gloucestershire village of Ampney St George. Beyond the village green, where three small girls were skipping over a rope in a desultory fashion, Neal turned up a narrow track and pulled into a cinder yard behind a row of farm cottages.

The back door of the end cottage swung open as he brought the Consul to a halt, and Neal emerged from the car to encounter a dumpy, rosy-cheeked woman of fifty bustling down the garden path to greet him.

"Why, Neal Gallian! What a lovely surprise! It's been too long, my dear, too long."

"Flo! Great to see you too. How are things?" Tall as he was, Neal was knocked back on his heels as Flo clattered into him and enveloped him in a fierce hug. He was aware of Jacko, who'd started to get out of the car, smirking with amusement.

"You must come in before you say another word," Flo declared. She noticed Jacko. "And your friend too, of course. What's your name, dear?"

Before Neal could sound a note of caution, Jacko had introduced himself, and he and Flo shook hands heartily.

"Flo Ormsby, dear. Young Neal lodged with me and my husband when he was with the p'lice in Cirencester, oh, years ago now. So, what brings you all this way today? Out for a nice ride in the country?"

As if it could have been that simple. "We came here because we need your help, Flo," Neal said.

"Well, it's yours, lovey. You don't even have to ask. But come inside, do, and I'll get the kettle on."

Flo hustled them across the yard, up the garden path and into a small, busy kitchen with an ancient range, and a table and four chairs crammed into a corner. She led them through – "Mind the step, dears," – to a cosy sitting room with the sofa and deep armchairs Neal remembered so well, the Welsh dresser containing the crockery Flo had inherited from her mum – "A wedding present to her and Dad, right back in 1905, it was, when they were married in St Michael's church just up the road." There was, too, the clumsy wireless in its walnut casing on the sideboard; and, of course, Ron, almost a fixture in the chair by the fireplace.

Ron looked up, saw Neal and raised his eyebrows. "Swipe me, look what the cat dragged in. What brings you back here after so long, then, boy?"

Ron was a beanpole of a man, bald, unsmiling and crafty, always out for what he could get. Neal had rubbed along with him well enough and was sure Ron and Jacko would get on like a house on fire.

"Neal and his friend here need our help," Flo told him in a voice which would brook no argument. She was going to help – always would – even though she hadn't a clue as to what sort of help would be needed.

"I just wondered if you'd mind putting Jacko up for a few days?" Neal explained. "You see -."

"Mind?" Both Ormsbys exclaimed the word at the same time, but Flo's indignant screech drowned out Ron's peevish utterance.

"'Course we wouldn't mind," Flo went on staunchly. "Any friend of yours, my duck." She silenced her husband's muted protest with a steely glare, and he subsided scowling into his chair.

Neal had decided not to tell them the whole truth. As far as the Ormsbys were concerned, he was still on the force. They'd read about the shooting, and Flo had visited him in the Radcliffe. He'd kept in spasmodic touch, once he was out of hospital, but if he told her of his current situation, she'd only fret, so on the way there he'd primed Jacko to maintain the fiction.

"Mr Manning's an important witness," he said, grateful that Jacko had assumed a deadpan expression. "The Super thinks it'd be best if he spends the few days before the trial in a place where he can't be contacted."

"How much is it worth?" Ron piped up, quickly silenced by another glare from his wife.

"He'll be fine here," Flo said reassuringly. "As long as he won't mind using our old caravan just up the track, around the back of the house?"

"That'd suit me down to the ground, Mrs Ormsby," Jacko enthused, with a conspiratorial grin at Neal.

"No problem, my dear," came the reply. "And you must call me Flo. He's Ron, for what it's *worth*."

"Hope it'll be worth something," Ron muttered darkly.

Flo turned her back on him in contempt. "I'll take you up there in a bit," she went on. "It's all clean and tidy, and the bed's aired. We have the occasional holidaymaker over the summer, but it's free at the moment. Otherwise there's a bed in the loft, though I dare say Mr Manning will prefer a bit of privacy?"

"It's Jacko," Jacko said with a broad grin.

"Jacko, then. You'll be more comfortable in the caravan, I should say."

Neal stifled a grin: he'd be out of Ron's way there. Because in Flo's opinion, Ron would have a bad influence on a saint; and Neal didn't reckon Jacko for a saint.

Flo swept on, clapping her hands heartily. "Now that's all sorted, you'll sit and have a mug of coffee and some of my dough cake. And Neal can tell us how he's been getting on since we last set eyes on him."

She turned, beaming, towards him, and he felt shamed by her generosity, because he knew he was about to be untruthful again. There were times when deception could be a necessary evil, but it pained him to lie to Flo. She'd been good to him, like a mother, at a time when his own mother had passed on, a time when he was vulnerable, coming into a job of which his stern father barely approved, and with the memory of his beloved elder brother fading farther away into the mist, as each year went by. He'd been the son Flo had never had, always ready to help with the chores on his days off; because she'd had little help from Ron, who'd either been at work on the neighbouring farm or, more likely, down at the village pub at every opportunity.

They'd been a good couple of years, and Neal had kept in touch, popping down at weekends after he'd transferred to Oxford. But then he'd met Clyde and Helen, and life had taken a different turn.

So, he told her how things were, hating himself for every word he uttered. Not much to report; yes, he'd recovered from the shooting, had got off lightly, working at a desk job at the moment; and no, Flo, sorry – no young lady on the horizon…

By midday, Ron had shuffled off to the pub, and Neal took his leave, assuring Flo he'd be back for Jacko by the middle of the week. Jacko followed him out to the car, once Neal had hugged Flo and thanked her for her kindness.

"Real diamond you are, Mr G," Jacko grinned. "What are you up to now, then?"

"I'm going to find Stoker and pick up where we left off last night, this time in private. I wouldn't mind betting he knows who was driving that van. As for you, Jacko, I want you to lie low – no wandering off, and keep away from the pub. I'll be back in a couple of days."

"Oh, have no fear, Mr G. Mother Flo'll keep me in order, I'll be bound."

"I dare say she will."

They shook hands, and Neal set off for Oxford. As he picked his way through the lanes to the main road, he felt the need for caution was greater than ever. Jacko Manning might well be in danger, but so was he. After all, Neal was the one asking the questions.

And he felt sure there was someone out there who didn't want him to find the answers.

7

He hadn't been back long when he heard the thump of Mrs Pendle's flat feet on the stairs, the prelude to her beating a solemn tattoo on his door.

He pulled it open to find her standing there wearing her best acid-drop expression.

"Telephone for you down in the hall, Mr Gallian. It's some young woman. I trust you weren't intending to invite her here? You know my Rules."

"Of course, Mrs Pendle. That's taken as read." The line of least resistance was always the best policy where his esteemed landlady was concerned, because it avoided a polemic. Besides, Neal wanted to get to the phone and find out who was calling him. Phone calls were a rarity, particularly from young women.

It was Jill Westmacott, sounding shy and a little distant. "Oh, Mr Gallian – Neal – Uncle Lam asked me to contact you." She lowered her voice to an anxious whisper. "They found Ted Stoker's body earlier this morning, a little way down the Windrush from Steenhampton."

"How did he die?" Neal was taken aback but succeeded in keeping his voice level.

"We assume he must have drowned. Uncle wondered if you'd want to come out to the cottage? He'll drive you to the spot. Sergeant Tomkins is over there at the moment."

Neal wasn't going to turn down the opportunity. "I'll be right over," he said. "Thanks for letting me know."

He replaced the receiver to find Mrs Pendle hovering at the foot of the stairs, pretending to dust the banister. She looked at him questioningly: it had probably sounded disappointingly business-like to her.

"Got to dash," he said tersely. "Someone's just died."

Mrs Pendle gasped, and Neal grinned as he turned away. It served her right for trying to eavesdrop. He ran upstairs, scooped up his car keys and told his goggle-eyed landlady that he'd be back later. She had the good grace to emerge from her trance and wish him luck.

In truth, as he hurried up the street to his car, Neal felt elated. Not because Stoker was dead – indeed, he'd much rather Stoker had stayed alive at least long enough to be interviewed again. It was because things were moving, and he wondered if Jacko Manning would be pleased to know that he'd stirred something up. Probably not, because he wouldn't be out of danger until Neal had discovered the van driver's identity. Might the same man be responsible for Ted Stoker's sudden demise? And how might it connect to Roger?

He made good time to Briar Hedge, where Colonel Wilkie greeted him heartily. The aroma of Sunday roast hung on the air, and Neal sniffed it nostalgically, knowing that Flo Ormsby would have offered readily, except that he'd not wanted to hang around. For his sins, he'd eat later: a tin of stewing beef and mashed potato.

Jill Westmacott was washing up in the kitchen and, on hearing his voice, came out to say hello, drying her hands on a tea towel. Neal thanked her again for phoning but was denied further conversation, as Wilkie ushered him into the sitting room, a hand at his shoulder. Jill, with an easy shrug, smiled and went back to her chores.

"Gallian, I asked Jill to contact you, because it seems too much of a coincidence. Bill Crannock phoned me with the news. He's given me the location, and we'll head out there now. Bill's gone with our local bobby, who's asked if he'll identify the body."

They set off, turning left halfway up Braxbury's High Street to pick up a road which ran parallel to the river valley. Two or three miles along it, Neal spotted an ambulance and a Hillman Minx with police markings parked up on the grass verge. As they drew nearer, he looked down across the meadows to see a small group of men clustered on the riverbank. Wilkie drew the Land Rover in behind the police car, and they climbed over the gate and made their way towards the gathering.

As they arrived, two ambulancemen were in the act of hefting a covered stretcher and, with a nod at the newcomers, bore it briskly away. That left a uniformed sergeant and a tall man standing with his back to them. They were deep in discussion but broke off as Wilkie approached.

"Afternoon, Colonel," the sergeant greeted him. "Bill here reckoned you might want to come along, being as the man had served under you and all. But it's done and dusted: police surgeon and photographer have been and gone, and Mr Crannock's in no doubt the poor unfortunate was Ted Stoker."

The tall man turned to acknowledge Wilkie. As he did so, Neal recognised with a start that he was the darts player whose hard scrutiny had seemed to spook Stoker at the Chasing Hound the previous evening. Neal had been walking behind Wilkie, had clocked the man before he could be seen himself. As Wilkie made the introductions, and the tall man came face to face with him, Neal was gratified to see him momentarily taken aback.

"Sergeant Tomkins is based in the police station at the top of Braxbury High Street," Wilkie explained, as the men faced each other. "And Bill Crannock served with me during the war."

By now, Crannock had ironed out his expression and offered his hand, his grip firm to the point of uncompromising. It summed him up, a dour, weather-beaten man of upright bearing, his hair short and grizzled at the temples. His expression might have been carved from stone.

Neal had never met Tomkins but had heard of him. He'd been at Braxbury for years. He had the reputation as a copper who made all the right noises, having got used to a quiet country existence over the years, with cosy retirement not so far away. He was smartly turned out in a crisp uniform and highly polished boots, but the eyes beneath his peaked cap were watchful. The type, Neal thought, who'd be distrustful of strangers on his patch. Strangers like him.

"Who found the body?" Wilkie asked.

The corner of Tomkins' mouth twitched in a cynical smile. "Mrs Peat from Blackberry Farm. She was on her way to church in Steenhampton and, as it was a nice morning, thought she'd walk there across the fields. Doubt if she'll do that again in a hurry. When she got on the blower to me, all hysterical-like, saying she found a body floating in the river, I wondered if it might not be our Ted. He lived just down the road in Marlford St John and often staggered back along the towpath after a session in the Hound. Right after that, Bill here got in touch with me, and we'd been thinking along the same lines."

"I'd got Ted a job at the chicken farm in Marlford, when he drifted back to this area." Crannock's voice was stern and clear. Neal could picture him as an NCO who'd stand no nonsense from his men. "Ben Tame, the owner, phoned me this morning. Ted was supposed to call in but hadn't shown up or returned to his lodgings. He'd had a skinful in the Hound last night." For the briefest moment, Crannock flicked a wary glance at Neal, then looked away. "So, I called Tommo here right away, and he'd just come off the phone to Mrs Peat."

"Accident waiting to happen," Tomkins commented lugubriously. "Ted had a reputation in these parts. Hauled him in myself a couple of times for being drunk and disorderly."

"He was certainly that last night," Crannock added. Again, the glance towards Neal. "I saw him. I was there."

Neal recognised the challenge and admired Crannock's honesty: the ex-sergeant wasn't one to hide away. More - he felt encouraged, lifted. For the first time, he started to believe there *was* something in all this and was determined to follow it through.

Crannock turned to face him, taking the initiative. "What's your interest in this, then, Mr Gallian? Did you know Ted?" The question was asked politely, but Neal detected an edge.

"I got talking to him only last night," he replied easily. "I stopped off at the Hound for a drink on my way home. I'd been visiting Colonel Wilkie."

"That's right." Wilkie was frowning, as if he sensed the tension.

"I'd heard that Mr Stoker had served under the colonel in France. I wanted to ask if he remembered my brother."

"You recall him, of course, don't you, Bill?" Wilkie cut in smoothly. "Roger Gallian, the young lieutenant up at the Chateau Garay."

Crannock nodded curtly. "Difficult to forget, sir." He turned back to Neal, his tone softening slightly. "I'm sorry about what happened, Mr Gallian. Your brother was a good officer, and I should know, having served under him."

Neal nodded his thanks, intended to reply, but Wilkie was in ahead of him. "As you know, Bill, we heard no news of Roger. But apparently Stoker had contacted Mr Gallian here with the notion that he might have some information concerning him."

Crannock looked sceptical. "And did he?" His keen gaze was trained on Neal's face.

Neal shrugged, deciding to play it down, give the impression he'd reached the end of the line. "If he did, he never shared it with me. He got cold feet and left in a hurry. He'd had plenty to drink, and I can't help thinking he'd hoped to spin a yarn and make a few quid out of me."

Crannock grinned mirthlessly. "Sounds like Ted, always on the make. I was his old sergeant, and he sought me out a few months ago. He was back in the area, down on his luck and looking for a job. My business is strictly a one-man show, but I found him something with Ben on his chicken farm in Marlford, and a room with an old lady in the village. Ted hadn't changed. Spent all he had on booze, and he'd try anything to supplement his earnings." His expression grew more serious. "I liked your brother, Mr Gallian. Nobody had a word to say against him. But I was there at the time, and the official version was the way it happened. Ted Stoker wouldn't have been able to add any more to it."

But Ted Stoker couldn't speak up for himself. Neal held on to that fact, as he murmured his thanks to Crannock.

Sergeant Tomkins had been listening to this exchange with interest, his gaze on Neal's face. "Thought your name sounded familiar. Aren't you a copper? One of the Oxford lot?"

As Neal turned towards him, he sensed Crannock's keen scrutiny. "Not anymore," he replied tersely.

"Something happened, I seem to recall? Couple of years back?"

Neal silently cursed Tomkins' persistence, knowing that Crannock was waiting on every word. He was aware of Wilkie, standing slightly aloof, looking on with helpless compassion.

"I was shot in the line of duty," he said stiffly. "A colleague – my best friend – was killed."

"Ah, I remember now. Some warehouse down by the Oxpens, wasn't it? Did they ever get the bloke?"

Would Tomkins never shut up? "No," Neal said. "They never did."

8

They never did…
    Tom Wrightson's voice still echoed in his head. "Are you receiving me?"
    "Loud and clear, Sarge."
    "Armed robbery, Gallian. Some villain just made off with the takings from Hobbs' store up the Cowley Road. Threatened the owner with a gun. Witness saw him get in a blue Ford van. Courtney and Thomas are on his tail, but he's weaving his way through the side streets. Might be heading for Marston and the by-pass."
    "Scrub that, Sarge. He's just shot past us in the High Street, heading in the opposite direction."
    "Okay, Gallian. Follow him. Keep me posted. I'll radio Courtney and get them to back you up. Listen, the bloke's nervous, and he's armed. Tell Holt no bleedin' heroics."
    Holt had heard, switched Neal that cunning glance. "Let's nab the bastard, Gally." He gunned the Humber squealing away from the kerb and set off down the High Street, siren shrilling furiously.
    "There he goes. Down Queen Street." Holt's voice pulsated with excitement. "Where d'you reckon he's heading?"
    "Botley or Oxpens."
    "My money's on Oxpens. Those warehouses next to the railway lines. He'll ditch the van and try to escape across the tracks."
    "I'll call it in." Neal grabbed the receiver. "Heading down Oxpens, Sarge. Hollybush Row."
    "Warehouses by the railway." Wrightson was ahead of him. "Courtney's in St Clement's. I'll send them after you. Take care, Gallian."
    "Will do, Sarge."
    There was little traffic about at that time of night, and Holt was gaining on the van. He sat crouched over the steering wheel, foot flat on the accelerator, absorbed in the chase. Halfway down the Oxpens, they caught the van's taillights, as it swung violently off to the right, down a narrow lane which ended in a cluster of warehouses.
    Dead end.
    Clyde Holt grinned triumphantly. "Got him now."

There was no way the van driver could have missed realising they were on his tail and closing. Clyde had been right. He'd abandon the van and head back across the tracks, try to escape that way.

They saw him, caught in their headlights as they swung on to the bumpy tarmac in front of the warehouses. He was too far away for them to be able to make out his features, but as soon as they appeared, he was off on foot, leaving the driver's door flapping open. His silhouetted figure blundered away down the strip of concrete between two of the units, beyond which lay another warehouse. Clyde skidded to a halt and leapt out.

"Wait!" Neal's voice was urgent: *a foreboding?*

"He's getting *away*." A flash of temper from Clyde, inevitable these days. He had something to prove, and Neal didn't know what it was. He wondered if even Clyde knew.

"We need back up."

"You turning yellow? Buster and Taff'll soon be here. Come *on!*"

Neal heaved open his door and stumbled out. "Down between those two front buildings, Clyde."

"I saw him." Impatient now. "Got the flashlight?"

"It's here."

"Give it me." He snatched it away.

Clyde led, the beam cavorting on the walls before them. Neal followed on closely, watchful. Another strident siren told them Courtney and Thomas weren't far behind.

"In here." A door at the side of the first warehouse stood slightly ajar. "We've got him." Holt's voice oozed triumph, as he gently pushed open the door.

Did they get him? Tomkins had asked.

*

Neal shook the memories away, but every word had left an echo, every movement a flickering image on his mind's tarnished silver screen.

He believed Tomkins read that, perhaps caught a glimpse of his pain, because he turned deliberately towards Crannock, his back to Neal. "I'd better get on. Drop you back, Bill?"

"Please, mate." Crannock's other option had been a ride back with Neal and Wilkie: Neal guessed he'd not want that. "All finished here, anyway." He allowed himself a brief, shifty glance towards Neal, then looked away.

"I presume there'll be an inquest?" Wilkie addressed his question to Tomkins.

"In a few days or so, Colonel. I need to track down Stoker's next of kin, presuming there is someone. I'll speak to Ben Tame too: he'll have to find himself a replacement. Well, that's about all we can do. I'll bid you good afternoon, Colonel, Mr Gallian."

He set off towards the road. Crannock followed, according the others a tight grin.

Wilkie waited until they were well ahead, then indicated that they should follow on. Tomkins and Crannock were well out of earshot, but the colonel kept his voice low. "I should imagine the memories never go away," he murmured sympathetically.

"No, sir. They don't."

*

"He's in here somewhere," Clyde hissed. "Come on, Gally, step on it."

Clyde in the lead: he always was. He'd been disciplined before for his gung-ho approach. Neal was his antithesis; erred on the side of caution. They'd complemented one another well.

Until now.

The warehouse was vast and echoing. Piles of wooden crates and cardboard boxes stretched along the far side, obscuring the windows. From beyond them came a desperate, scrabbling noise.

"He's at a window!" Clyde charged forward. Neal had read his intention, had caught up and placed a steadying hand on his shoulder. Clyde shook it off, kept moving.

The warehouse was unlit, only the light of the moon filtering through the skylights. In a gap between two stacks of crates, Neal suddenly glimpsed the blacker-than-darkness shape of the gun.

"Clyde!" he bawled. "His gun! Get down!"

His words bounced off the bare brick walls, and time froze. And there it was again, each and every time, with every moment when he was jarred into wakefulness, when he paused to let the memories rise up in deadly ambush. Again. *Again:* I could have saved him…

I could have saved him, if I'd had my wits about me, had my brain not frozen at that vital moment, had I not somehow found myself wading through cloying, glutinous mud; allowing those imperative fractions of seconds to stutter by, as I poised to launch myself and dash him out of the sight of the murderous, levelling gun...

He was airborne, but too late, far, far too late; heard the boom, saw Clyde check his stride, the force of the shot slamming him backwards. Clyde's flailing arm snatched at cardboard boxes, brought them tumbling down on top of himself, as he pitched over to sprawl helplessly on the floor, the flashlight vaulting from his grasp to land, shatter and roll forlornly away.

Neal, on his knees, looked up, saw through that gap a clear path to a small window, which the fugitive had wrenched open, saw the man's lower torso scrambling through the aperture. He started to get up, and the man, who'd made it outside now, saw him.

Neal had the briefest glimpse of a face, thin, pale, terrified; saw the booming gun again, realised too late that it was pointed directly at him. The explosion almost deafened him, and in the next instant he felt his shoulder being ripped apart, found himself falling, spiralling down with box after box raining upon him, inviting the searing blackness.

His last recollection was of that face, its frightened expression. It was a face he'd never forget, a face which didn't register among the mug shots in CID files, which he carefully and tearfully pored over many empty weeks later.

"Did they get him?"
"No, they never did..."

*

"So many bad memories," Lambert Wilkie was saying, as they walked back to his Land Rover. "It's so difficult, isn't it, to put it all behind us?"

"Yes," he replied tersely. "It is."

He switched Wilkie a glance, recognised his look of compassion. Wilkie had been referring to Roger, of course, not Clyde. But Neal wasn't ready to talk about Clyde; not then, perhaps not ever.

Then it hit him that Wilkie must have suffered too. All those years in the army, particularly the war years, he who'd known the names of each of his men, he would have suffered loss too, many losses. It would be equally difficult for Wilkie to put it all behind him, or ever to forget.

Neal snapped out of his black mood, as the colonel nodded in the direction of Tomkins' Hillman, now a quarter of a mile up the road.

"Our sergeant's no ball of fire," he said. "It's done and dusted in his book, certainly as far as poor Stoker is concerned. Death by misadventure, accident while under the influence, any similar convenient verdict."

"And you're not sure?"

Wilkie turned a searching glance on him. "No, Gallian, I'm not. I don't see how, I really don't. But I'm starting to believe there's something in this."

"It started with Roger," Neal said, recognising the hint of hope in his own voice. "Might Stoker have known something after all?" He made the impromptu decision to confide in Wilkie. He'd found the colonel sympathetic all along, added to which the man was a realist, with a long and notable Army career behind him.

Neal told him about his meeting with Manning two nights before. For him, that had been the starting point.

"He's a petty crook I ran in a while back," he explained. "He's a likeable enough chap, reckons he's going straight now."

"Oh, right." A half-smile from Wilkie.

"Precisely. With someone like Jacko, you can never be sure." He told Wilkie about their close call with the van at the Chasing Hound the previous evening; and how he'd arranged for Jacko to lay up somewhere safe for a couple of days.

"Where does Manning fit into this?" Wilkie asked, curious.

"He was in the Army with Stoker earlier in the war. North Africa, I believe."

The colonel nodded thoughtfully. "Ah, that'd be it. I knew he wasn't one of my crew."

"But Bill Crannock was."

Wilkie drew to a halt, struck by Neal's tone. "Yes, that's right. What of it?"

Sensing an element of defensiveness in the colonel's manner, he told him about Crannock's presence at the Chasing Hound, and how Stoker had seemed spooked by him.

Wilkie looked pained as they walked on. "Bill was a good NCO," he said. "I've never had reason to doubt his honesty. His business went belly-up a few years back. He came to me, and I helped him set up a carrier business in Braxbury. I'm thinking it's more likely he and Stoker had history. Stoker had a reputation as a waster, and that wouldn't have gone down well with Bill."

Neal decided to leave it there. Perhaps Wilkie was right, although he couldn't bring himself to agree.

They avoided the subject on the way back to Braxbury. Wilkie said that he'd be out for most of the following day: a long lunch in Cheltenham with ex-army colleagues. But he'd give some thought to all they'd discussed, and they'd resume their conversation in the near future.

The men shook hands firmly as they parted. Neal returned to Oxford in a lighter frame of mind. He'd previously hoped Wilkie would prove an ally: he felt sure of it now.

9

Neal headed back to Steenhampton the next morning. Ted Stoker had been pretty much in his cups when he'd met him, and he supposed it was hardly surprising that he'd drowned. An excess of alcohol combined with a walk home along a riverbank didn't bode well; even so, Neal wondered if he'd had a helping hand. And if he had, that gave rise to the possibility that Stoker really had known something with regard to Roger. On top of that, Neal distrusted the sinister presence of Bill Crannock.

He decided not to call in on Sergeant Tomkins: he and Crannock had seemed friendly, and he didn't want Crannock to get wind of his continued interest just yet. So, Neal returned to the Chasing Hound to speak with the landlord. He'd just opened up and was happy to have a chat with his first customer of the day.

The landlord reckoned he'd known Ted Stoker as well as anyone. He'd come to the area two years back, down on his luck, thanks to his fondness for liquor. Bill Crannock, his old sergeant from army days, had fixed him up with a job at Ben Tame's chicken farm down the road in Marlford St John and found him lodgings with old Mrs Fairbairn in Swan Lane. Only trouble was the booze. Not that the landlord was complaining, but Stoker must have spent every spare ha'penny on it. He'd been a morose sort of bloke who didn't mix easily, and the landlord couldn't think of anyone he'd been particularly friendly with.

Ben Tame couldn't add much to that. Stoker did his job, didn't say a lot, seemed hung-over most of the time; although until that last morning, he'd always turned up for work, whatever the day or hour.

And Neal drew another blank with Mrs Fairbairn. She was a decent old soul of nearly eighty and, having lost her husband some years back, she'd been grateful for the chance of a paying lodger. She knew 'poor Mr Stoker' had been 'rather fond of his ale', but as she always went to bed early and slept deeply, she was never disturbed by his coming back so late most evenings. Stoker had kept himself to himself, had never had any callers and very little in the way of post.

"The gentleman who called here must have been a friend of his, though," Mrs Fairbairn concluded.

Neal's interest was immediately aroused. "What did he want?" he asked.

"Oh, he called to pass on his condolences. He said he'd known Mr Stoker for many years and wondered if he might have a look in his room to see if there was an address for a next of kin. Said he was calling on behalf of Sergeant Tomkins."

"Did you recognise this man, Mrs Fairbairn?" Neal felt he already did.

"A tall man with short, dark hair. Oh, I've seen him around a lot. I believe he's the Braxbury carrier."

Bill Crannock. Neal wondered what he might have been looking for? And why wouldn't Tomkins have called in himself? It seemed lax on the sergeant's part, which didn't surprise Neal; but in Tomkins' book, the death of Ted Stoker wouldn't rate highly anyway.

However, did Crannock's visit confirm Neal's suspicion that Stoker had had something to tell him about Roger after all? *And that Crannock was keen to suppress it?*

He thanked Mrs Fairbairn and drove back to Oxford in a thoughtful mood. It was getting well on into the afternoon when he arrived, to find Mrs Pendle waiting in gleeful ambush behind the kitchen door.

"That young woman of yours telephoned earlier," she announced. "I said I didn't know when you'd be back. She left her number and asked for you to ring when you returned." Mrs Pendle sniffed disapprovingly. "You can call from here, as long as you leave fourpence on the tray."

She'd written the number on the pad beside the phone. Neal presumed the caller had been Jill Westmacott but didn't recognise the number as that of Briar Hedge. Under Mrs Pendle's all-seeing eye, he dug a penny and threepenny bit out of his trouser pocket, deposited them on the tray and dialled, switching his landlady a stern glance. Realising his unspoken request for privacy, she shuffled a respectful distance away, while still managing to remain within earshot.

The call was answered on the second ring, and Jill's hesitant voice informed him that he'd reached Vernon's Wine Store in Braxbury.

"Hello, Jill? Neal Gallian."

"Oh, Neal, thank goodness." Her relief was evident. "Thanks for calling back. Uncle Lam's out all day and won't be home till late. I need some advice, and I thought of you. I'm really sorry to bother you."

"It's no bother at all. What's the problem?"

"Something happened earlier, which has left me feeling uncomfortable. A man called here, asking to see Mr Vernon. Well, he's away on business, which isn't unusual, and his wife, who runs the shop, has gone up to London for the day…"

He could tell that she was agitated. "And you think there's something suspicious about this man?"

He heard her intake of breath. "My goodness! How did you guess?"

"Force of habit," he replied with a grin.

"Oh, of course. Silly me. You see, he was a very scruffy little man. I really didn't like him at all. I think he could see that, and it amused him. He'd drawn up in the yard in a battered old van, and to my mind he didn't fit into the category of one of Mr Vernon's usual customers. I told him to come back tomorrow. At least Mrs Vernon will be here, and she can soon sort him out if necessary."

"And did he agree to do that?"

"Well, he did, with a sly grin on his face. Before he returned to the van, he walked around the yard, taking a good look at the outbuildings. That's where Mr Vernon stores boxes of wine, and quite honestly, the man was acting suspiciously."

"Do you think he might come back later?"

"Well, yes – yes, I'm worried that he might."

"What time do you close?"

"Five-thirty. Just over an hour from now."

"Are either of the Vernons likely to be back this evening?"

"Mrs Vernon, maybe. But she often stays away for the night when she goes on one of her shopping trips."

"Lock up at five-thirty, and I'll pick you up from the shop. Once it's dark, we'll go back into Braxbury to make sure everything's secure."

"Oh, Neal, would you? It'd be such a weight off my mind."

"I'll see you in an hour, then."

"That's wonderful. Thank you. I -er, I'll cook you some tea. Er, that's if -?"

"I'd appreciate that. Oh, Jill? This man – did you recognise him?"

"He's no-one I've ever seen before. Short, plump, scruffy, about mid-forties. Oh, and he was wearing a dirty green hat."

Neal thanked her and ended the call, trying to subdue his sudden elation.

A man in a green hat: just like the spectator at the darts match, two nights before at the Chasing Hound.

The man who'd been in conversation with Bill Crannock.

10

Jill was clearly relieved to see him when he drew up outside the shop late that afternoon.

"Sorry to drag you out here," she apologised, as she got into the car beside him. "I dare say it's just me being silly. But I was suspicious of him."

"He sounds rather unsavoury," Neal replied. "And first instincts are often the right ones. We'll come back here after dark and take a look. As it's Monday, I imagine it'll be a quiet night in Braxbury. That might encourage him to turn up early."

They drove back to Briar Hedge. As expected, Colonel Wilkie still hadn't returned, and Jill immediately set about preparing them a meal. Neal had only stopped briefly for a sandwich earlier in the day and felt he was ready for something more substantial. He insisted on helping her out, peeling a few potatoes and putting them on to boil, while she sorted out some vegetables to go with the cold gammon and brewed the tea.

Jill came across as a serious sort of girl, rather shy, and Neal guessed she'd not had a lot of contact with the outside world. He was surprised but flattered at the way she'd taken him, virtually a stranger, on trust and invited him into her home, which was miles from anywhere. But he supposed the incident in the shop that afternoon had unnerved her, and she was relieved to have company. They fell into conversation as they sat over their meal at the kitchen table.

Once she'd finished her teacher training, Jill had gone out to Kenya to join her parents, who were both teachers. They'd encouraged her to follow them into the profession, but she wasn't sure it was what she really wanted. She'd been glad of the opportunity to return to England and keep house for her uncle, while she decided on the next step.

Neal didn't give away much about himself. He sketched over the warehouse incident and explained how, once he'd recovered, he couldn't face returning to the police force. The memories had been too painful, and currently he seemed to be drifting from job to job. He didn't say it, but they seemed to have something in common: the need to get their lives together.

Jill heard him out sympathetically. He felt she wanted to ask him to go into more detail. But she was too reserved, too reluctant to ask, and he was glad of that, because he didn't want to inflict it on her. She'd asked for his help and put her trust in him. He decided to keep it on that level. He couldn't bear to tell her more, in case he might alienate her.

Their meal over, he suggested they make a move, for darkness had set in. He advised her to wear something warm: it might be a long vigil, and the night promised to be a cold one. Jill had already thought of that, slipping a sheepskin coat over a thick cardigan.

They drove into Braxbury, parked near the top of the almost deserted High Street and walked back down to the wine shop. Only the pubs were open, with a handful of customers inside, and they passed no-one in the street.

Jill had explained the layout as they'd travelled. The wine shop fronted on to the High Street, but there was also a side entrance situated next to Vernon's storage shed and garage. A wide driveway lay to the side of the shop, and at its far end was the Vernons' house, The Leylands, hidden from the road by a tall leylandii hedge.

As soon as Neal saw it, he told Jill they'd conceal themselves behind the hedge, as they'd have a good view of the shed and the shop's side entrance. He didn't think Green Hat would wait too long, if burglary was his objective.

They took up their positions and waited. Almost immediately, Neal began to feel uncomfortable. He'd been on stakeouts a number of times during his years on the force, but even though the surrounding buildings were in darkness, he was unable to dismiss the feeling that someone else was present. He concentrated on listening but heard nothing.

He said nothing to Jill. In any case, they'd agreed not to speak at all, unless it was a matter of urgency. Despite the thickness of her sheepskin coat, he sensed that she was suppressing a shiver. He wondered about putting an arm around her but didn't want her to get the wrong impression.

Suddenly, she gasped as the beam of headlights raked the forecourt, and Neal felt her tense, as a small van growled towards them to halt no more than two or three yards away. The clashing of gears followed, and the van whined away in reverse to back up to the storage shed doors, where the driver cut the lights. Peering cautiously through the branches of a bush, Neal tried to make out if the driver was alone.

It seemed that he was, for only one man got out, closing his door softly. He was some distance away, a silhouette against the night, but Neal was sure it was the squat figure of the man he'd seen in the Chasing Hound. The hat perched on his head seemed to confirm it.

Then Jill tugged at his sleeve and pointed in the direction of the shed. A second figure had arrived and, as he spotted him, Neal tried to work out exactly where he'd come from. For he was suddenly there, and Neal guessed he'd been lying in wait for Green Hat. It explained his earlier suspicion that someone else had been nearby.

Was the second man aware of him and Jill? Had he seen them arrive? If he had, he gave no indication of having done so. The two men were discussing something in whispers. It was impossible to hear what they were saying. Also, in the darkness and a good twenty-five yards away, Neal was unable to make out their features. He turned to Jill and mouthed to her that they'd stay put and observe what happened next. He sensed her relief, as her hand found his.

They continued to watch, as the second man undid the padlock and opened the doors of the storage shed. At the same time, Green Hat pulled open the van's rear doors, and the two men went into the shed.

They weren't in there long. Neal saw shadows moving around, heard some grunting and a scuffling of feet, as things were loaded into the van. Then the doors of the shed were shut, and the padlock clicked back into place. Green Hat closed the van doors, got in behind the wheel and drove away, only switching on his headlights as he turned into the High Street.

Like Neal, Jill had been peering through the branches of the hedge. "Where did he go?" she whispered. "The second man? I must have missed him."

In the darkness, it had been difficult to see much at all. "I missed him as well," Neal whispered back. "He must have slipped away as suddenly as he'd appeared. And did you notice that he *unlocked* the padlock, so he must have had a key? Couldn't have been Vernon, I don't suppose?"

Jill shook her head. "Mr Vernon's a much bigger man. It definitely wasn't him. And where did the other one come from?"

"I'd guess he came from the street. He could easily have crept round without our seeing him." Neal paused, struck by a further thought. "Quite possibly he saw us arrive and knew we were there all the time."

Jill looked anxious. "What do you suggest we do?"

"Well, as we saw, he unlocked the shed, so unless he stole a key, no crime's been committed." He scrambled up and helped her to her feet, realising he'd not let go of her hand for the last ten minutes. But it was resting comfortably in his, so he didn't release it.

"Let me drive you home," he went on. "It's rather late, and your uncle will be worried."

"I left a note by his chair," she replied, smiling. "Knowing how these so-called lunches ramble on, it's likely he won't be there himself."

He returned the smile, looking carefully around as they walked out of the cover of the hedge. All that met him was silence. He felt certain the second man had gone, recognised his own tension, as he led Jill across the forecourt and out on to the street. She clung tightly to his hand, as they walked up the hill to his car.

They arrived back at Briar Hedge to find that Colonel Wilkie had returned, for the lights were on as Neal swung on to the drive and drew up beside the Land Rover. He reached across and opened the passenger door.

Jill laid a tentative hand on his sleeve. "Thank you, Neal," she said. "I was worried, but I imagine Mr Vernon may have arranged for a collection and forgot to tell me about it."

"Glad I could help," he said lightly, although the evening's events had stirred his suspicions.

"Sorry to have wasted your time," she added meekly.

"It wasn't wasted," he replied.

Her hand had remained on his sleeve. He placed his over hers. They moved hesitantly towards one another, lips touching briefly, shaping into a kiss. And then the cottage door swung open. A blaze of light illuminated them, and Wilkie appeared in the doorway. With a smile of apology – he hoped of regret too – Jill squeezed his arm and got out of the car.

They wished each other goodnight, Neal raised a hand in acknowledgement to Wilkie and drove away as they went inside.

Jill was in conversation with her uncle, and Neal assumed she was explaining where they'd been. He guessed she'd be dismissing the incident out of hand.

But for his part, his suspicions were aroused.

11

Neal drove back to Oxford in a thoughtful frame of mind. Everything that had happened that evening was pushed aside into a tiny waiting room at the back of his mind.

Everything except that kiss he'd shared with Jill.

As a kiss, it had been tentative, probing, the coming together of two uncertain, lonely people.

She was far too young for him anyway; barely into her twenties, while he was thirty-three. She'd scarcely begun to live, while he -? It was a good point: had *he* begun to live? He couldn't go there, wasn't ready; wondered if he'd ever be ready.

And in any case, that brief touching of lips had brought another dusty memory springing to the forefront of his mind: the last time he'd kissed a woman.

Helen.

*

He'd transferred to Oxford seven years previously, a fish out of water when he'd met Clyde, and a little later Helen. Cirencester had been a quiet berth, becoming predictable. He'd been a young man, three years on the force, not wanting to get stuck in a pleasant rut like some of his older colleagues, some of the rural coppers he'd met. He'd wanted something more, felt he owed it to his father.

Lionel Gallian had disapproved of his younger son joining the police. He'd expected Neal to join the Army, as he'd done, as Roger had done. But his term of National Service had convinced Neal that it wasn't the life for him. He'd chosen the police partly as a sop to his father and also because he'd wanted to be his own man. And Lionel, to be fair, had met him halfway on this, now and then taking an interest in his son's experiences.

The Cirencester years were comfortable. He'd moved out of the family home. By then, it could hardly be called a home, for his mother had died a while back, and Lionel spent much of his time morose and closeted with his memories: Roger's desertion had effectively destroyed them both.

Neal had lodged with the Ormsbys during his time at Cirencester. Flo had treated him like the son she'd never had, and he'd even had a fondness for unsmiling, money-grubbing old Ron. It had been *home*. But even so, he'd known that he needed to move on while he still could.

Oxford was busier, pacier, promising much with the eternal wrangling between town and gown, the overspill of villains from London and Birmingham. He realised straight away that he had a lot to learn, but he was a willing student. And Clyde Holt had quickly taken the new boy under his wing.

In many way, Clyde and Neal were opposites: Clyde robust, extrovert, always leading from the front and charging head-first into a situation to get a quick result; while Neal was cautious, wanting to think things through before committing himself.

But Clyde's endearing quality was that he was a true friend, and it soon became clear why Sergeant Wrightson – 'Uncle Tom' – had paired them up. They complemented each other well, made a good team. True, Neal was a bit green, but Clyde looked out for him, and he always made a point of watching Clyde's back.

Except that once…

*

Clyde and Helen weren't married when he first knew them. She worked as an invoice typist at Blackwell's in St Aldates, and Clyde had made a point of bumping into her when she went out at lunchtime, or when she was waiting in the bus queue at Carfax. Being Clyde, it didn't take him long to ask her out.

In the early days, Neal would tag along with them to the Ritz in George Street, the Regal in Cowley Road, to Saturday night dances where'd he'd sit out nursing a pint of warm, flat beer while they jived the night away. He'd have the occasional date himself, but these never came to anything, and he wasn't exactly nimble on the dance floor. He tried to convince himself that he preferred his own company but wondered if he was being quite honest.

Often Helen would take pity and dance with him. "Oh, come on, Neal, Clyde'll need to sit this one out – he can't keep up with me." He remembered one song, to him more memorable than the witless gyrating to *Rock around the Clock, Hound Dog,* and the like: a Nat King Cole number, *When I Fall in Love,* just a slow waltz, a haunting melody, as he held her close and wished he might hold her closer, trying desperately not to misplace his two left feet.

Helen, in her bright, full skirts, dark hair swishing about her shoulders as she jived, her laughing eyes, gleaming red lips…

Neal kept his distance: *she was Clyde's girl, and he was Clyde's best friend.* From early on in his life, he recalled his father drumming into him that he must strive to be an honourable man. Neal had seen that quality in Roger, always determined to emulate it, although Lionel never mentioned Roger now. Even though Roger was no longer an example. Even though Neal's emotions were tugging him in a direction he feared to take.

Eighteen months on, Clyde and Helen married. Neal was Clyde's best man, happy for them, and once they'd returned from honeymoon, he was a frequent dinner guest at their tiny Cutteslowe flat. By that time, he didn't see much of Clyde, who was ambitious for promotion and had a short spell in CID.

That didn't last. Within six months, Clyde was back in uniform, back with Neal on the squad cars.

He didn't say much about his time with CID, just that it "hadn't worked out." It was rumoured there'd been an incident: that he might have gone too far with a suspect and been hauled over the coals. Neal didn't wish to add to his pain, simply told Clyde that he'd be there if he ever wanted to talk, otherwise he'd not allude to it. Clyde thanked him warmly but never took up the invitation.

If anything, he became more impulsive. He was still ambitious; intended to stay in uniform and get his stripes. But unaccountably, he failed his sergeants' exam.

Then Clyde became frustrated, and his attitude went over the top. He'd always been extrovert, bursting with masculinity, a boxer, a hard-hitting rugby flanker; and one or two villains they'd collared had come in for a hard time.

Neal became anxious, spoke to his friend about it. "Pah! They're crooks, Gally. Low-lifes."

The victims complained now and again about their maltreatment. "That big bugger with the attitude laid into me for no reason!" The ACC and DCI Pilling interviewed Neal, but he played it down. "Holt might have been a bit over-enthusiastic, sir. But he never started it, I swear."

Hadn't he? Questionable, even though Clyde had been provoked: some of them knew how to get under his skin. But Neal wouldn't drop him in it, and Clyde was grateful for that. They were best mates, and Neal felt he owed him, because he'd looked after him, helped him find his feet, never excluded him. He wasn't going to snitch. Instead, he talked to him, tried to reason with him time and again. But it made little difference.

It soon got worse.

One day, not long before *it* happened, Clyde had been temporarily paired with another officer. "Hodgson's fairly new, and I need Holt to show him the ropes," Tom Wrightson had said. Clyde hadn't seemed happy with that, and Neal saw the ACC's hand in it. But he decided to use it to his advantage and, on his day off, went along to see Helen and ask her to have a timely word with her husband.

She invited him in but for once seemed reluctant to do so. He could tell she was in the middle of baking, as there were traces of flour on her hands and apron. But that wasn't the reason for her preoccupation.

Helen placed her cake in the oven, hung her apron over a chair and made them coffee. They sat in opposite armchairs, as they always did, either side of the two-bar electric fire. Neal broached the subject hesitantly, explaining that he felt it was in Clyde's best interests.

She heard him out distractedly, almost as if she wasn't properly listening, as if she didn't really want him there. Yes, yes, she'd have a word. For what good it would do.

Then she burst into tears. Helen, whom he'd never seen in any kind of distress before; vivacious, sweet-natured, optimistic Helen.

Neal leapt startled to his feet and approached her. She quickly turned her face away, but not before he'd seen her reason for doing so: an ugly purple bruise below her left eye.

He reached out and gently hauled her up from her chair. She offered no resistance.

"Helen, how did this happen?"

Finally, she turned her tearstained face towards him, looked him in the eye.

"I've told our neighbours I walked into a door. But I won't lie to you, Neal."

She must have seen the shock on his face. For a few moments, he was unable to form words; and when at last he did, they sounded woefully inadequate. "I know he's been under pressure recently. The CID thing, he's never spoken about it..."

His voice tailed away. She was shaking her head, her lip trembling. "It started after that. Something went wrong, and I'm not sure what. And it's not the first time. I've been able to cover it up before."

"I'll speak to him." His tone was decisive, his mood grim.

"*No!*" She reached out, clamped a hand on his arm. "No, Neal. These – these moods of his, they - they'll pass, I'm sure they will. He's just so frustrated with his job at the moment. Those months in CID – he won't talk about them, simply won't. He was upset. I'm sure that's why he failed the sergeant's exam." She looked up at him imploringly, clung more tightly to him. "You're a great friend to us both, Neal. Please, *please*, go on being that."

"But if it happens again?"

"It won't."

It did. And finally, Neal knew he had to speak out. He'd take Clyde aside once they came off duty that night, go to a pub, an all-night café, sit him down and get him to open up about what was troubling him.

But the opportunity never arose. For that was the night *it* happened.

And in any case, by then there was a further complication. Something else he had to tell Clyde, needed to: a confession, which, in the end, he was never able to make.

Helen in his arms, their faces inching tentatively closer, as they moved into that kiss which had been inevitable for so long.

*

And now, as he drove, approaching the Woodstock Road roundabout, the twinkling lights of the city drawing him in, he willed Helen Holt's image to fade away, to slip back into the dark library of memory. And yes, perhaps for Jill Westmacott's image to supersede it.

But Helen's remained, refused to leave. Almost as if she never could.

Almost as if it had never ended.

12

The urgent jangling of the telephone down in the hall awoke him the next morning. He glanced blearily at his bedside clock: just after seven. He heard Mrs Pendle answer it, her tone monosyllabic and bordering on belligerent, then the thump of her slippers on the stairs and an impatient tattoo on his door.

"Mr Gallian? You awake?" Her eldritch shriek might have woken the dead. "Phone call for you. Says it's urgent."

His first thought was of Jill. "Who is it?" he asked cautiously.

"Dunno. Didn't say. Some woman." She paused. "Old," she added grudgingly, sounding miffed at being deprived of an opportunity to draw his attention to her Rules.

Neal got out of bed and slipped a dressing gown over his pyjamas. Mrs Pendle stood on the landing, eyeing him suspiciously. He could read her mind. Whether the caller was old or not, that made two female callers in two days. In Mrs Pendle's blinkered eyes, it bordered dangerously on licentiousness.

He thanked her, doubting she'd be mollified, and went down to the hallway.

"Hello?"

"Oh, Neal, thank the Lord!" It was Flo Ormsby, in a right taking, which probably hadn't been soothed by her recent verbal clash with Mrs Pendle.

"What's wrong, Flo?" His words sounded calm but didn't reflect the way he was feeling inside. As soon as he heard Flo's voice, he knew it couldn't be good news.

Flo's next utterance confirmed it. "He's *gone*. Your friend – he's *gone*."

"Jacko gone? What – just walked out?"

Flo managed to collect herself a little. "No, Neal. I don't reckon he did it by himself."

Alarm bells rang deafeningly. "I'm coming over right away." Cutting short Flo's gasp of relief, he replaced the receiver and ran back up the stairs, past Mrs Pendle, who'd taken up her favourite listening post on the bottom stair.

"Sounds as if something's up," she remarked ghoulishly, as he charged into his room.

"Life and death, Mrs P," he called back viciously, not waiting around for an answer. She stared at him speechlessly as he raced past a couple of minutes later, soon out of the reach of further questions.

On this occasion, Neal took a more direct route to Ampney St George. He had no concerns now about being followed, feeling that any damage might already have been done. Traffic was busy in central Oxford, but once clear of St Giles, he had a good run and had reached the village within the hour. Flo was waiting at the cottage's front gate, looking anxious, her plump hands twisting her apron distractedly.

"Oh, Neal. Thank goodness you're here."

"When did he leave?" he asked, as he followed her inside.

"That's just the point." Flo's worried expression darkened. "He went off last night – and that useless lump Ormsby didn't say anything about it until this morning!"

They went through to the kitchen, where Ron was mulling lugubriously over a bowl of cornflakes. He threw Neal a guilty up-from-under look. "Mornin', young Gallian."

Flo stood over him, arms folded formidably. "He was on his way back from the pub last night," she declared. "About ten, wasn't it?"

"Nearer half-nine," Ron corrected indignantly. "Never stay long, y'see. Flo don't like it."

"And you're always half-sozzled in any case," Flo accused him. "Go on, you tell Neal what you saw."

"Well, this van come past me in the village street, see. I thought it must've turned up the track here but couldn't be sure. Driver had cut the lights. Then I heard voices arguing. I couldn't hear the words, 'cos they wasn't talking loud or nothin'. And I never thought no more about it. I mean, why should I?"

Flo's baleful expression was enough to tell him why he should. Ron looked up warily for permission to continue, but his wife barged in ahead of him.

"I went up there this morning to see if Mr Manning'd like some breakfast. Door was on the latch, so I went in. Well, he'd gone. No sign of him anywhere. So, I come back here, only for *him* to tell me he must've gone last night."

"The van come back past me, see," Ron resumed defensively. "It was so dark, I never seen nothing. Two people in the cab, and off it sped away and out of the village."

"Did you see either of the figures?" Neal asked.

"Just their sillerettes, like. Van only had its sidelights on, and there's no street lighting."

"So, you didn't get the number?" Neal spoke without hope, and Flo was already staring at the ceiling in exasperation.

Ron shook his head. "Sorry, young Gallian. Never thought nothing of it. But it was one of them small Morris vans, as I recall. Though it might have been a Commer."

The alarm bells were ringing even louder, especially when Flo produced a crumpled scrap of paper from the pocket of her apron.

"Mr Manning must have left this," she said. "I found it in the bedroom up at the caravan this morning. He'd left it under the pillow."

Neal took hold and studied it. It was written in a heavy scrawl, and probably in something of a hurry. *'Tell Mr G got called away. Wife's not too good. He'll understand.'*

Flo was frowning. "P'raps after all it was a friend come and picked him up, someone who knew his poor wife had been took bad?"

She didn't sound too sure, and Neal didn't want to alarm her. "That may well be it, Flo," he replied. "Leave it with me. I'll check up on it."

He knew full well it wasn't. Jacko had told Neal as much himself: *he wasn't married.* The note had been his way of letting Neal know that he'd not left willingly.

Despite his precautions, he figured that he and Manning must have been followed to Ampney St George the other day. He thought he'd been watchful, but obviously not watchful enough. He cursed himself for being so out of touch.

He had to make light of it in front of the Ormsbys. He told them that Jacko should have let him know, rather than leave a note and dash off; but if his wife was ill, he could understand why he'd done so. He offered to settle up for Jacko's board and lodging, and Ron, emerging from his cornflakes, perked up eagerly at the prospect of beer money.

Flo quickly squashed it. "You owe us *nothing*, my dear. It's been good to have you here again, and you must promise to call again soon."

Neal promised and, out of pity, held out to Ron a ten-shilling note for his next trip to the pub. Flo deftly snatched it from between Ron's twitching fingers and stuffed it into Neal's shirt pocket. "Ormsby drinks too much anyway," she grumbled.

Flo stood at the gate waving Neal off until he was out of sight, but once Ampney St George was behind him, the black mood descended. He feared for Manning's well-being.-Ron had thought the van might have been a Commer or a Morris: they looked quite similar. Just like the other night at the Chasing Hound and in Steenhampton. "He's out to get *me*," Jacko had whined. Neal wondered if he already had.

On impulse, he drove up to Birmingham, having traced the company Jacko worked for from a directory in a garage on the A38. Herbert Bolsover was a vast, distressingly cheerful man, wedged firmly behind a desk in an office above a brewery. He'd given Jacko his chance once he'd come out of prison, and the little ex-con seemed to have grasped it with both hands. Bolsover got on fine with him, and Jacko was well-liked by the customers on his patch.

Bolsover confirmed that Jacko had telephoned him out of the blue two days previously to ask if he could take some overdue holiday. He had no idea where he might have gone and had heard nothing from him since, but promised he'd contact Neal if he did.

He supplied the address of Jacko's lodgings, but the landlady hadn't seen him for almost a week. Her main concern was that she needed to know if he wasn't coming back, so that she could rent out the room.

She pointed Neal in the direction of the Horse and Cart a couple of streets away. Jacko was a good customer there, and perhaps Lil or one of the regulars might know where he'd be likely to have gone.

Lil was a busty blonde barmaid of forty-something, and Neal guessed that if anyone might have information about Jacko's whereabouts, she'd be the one. But Lil was as clueless as the rest of the regulars. 'Old Jacko' was the life and soul of any party, particularly the Saturday night singsongs, and they looked forward to his return.

"Gone away on holiday, has he? Never said a dickie bird to anybody about that." Lil sounded peeved. "Just wait till I see him. I'll give him a piece of my mind."

As he drove back to Oxford, Neal wondered whether she'd ever get the opportunity.

13

He might have had doubts before but, as he drove back from Birmingham late that afternoon, Neal admitted he had none now. Jacko Manning had lit the fuse when he'd met him in the Farmers four nights previously, and Neal was convinced that it was all to do with Roger. Roger, alive or dead, in France or some other part of the world, was involved in this. But he had no idea as to how or why, and knew he had to follow it through.

He needed to talk things over with Colonel Wilkie and headed for Briar Hedge. It was after six o'clock when he drove down Braxbury High Street, and he was surprised to spot Jill Westmacott waiting alone at a bus stop halfway down the hill and looking anxious. He pulled into the kerb and wound down the window. "Jill?"

She saw him, and her face broke into a smile. "Neal! Back in Braxbury so soon?"

"I'm on my way to have a word with your uncle. Hop in, and I'll give you a lift."

Jill got in. "I hope he's there," she said. "He was supposed to pick me up from the shop at five-thirty. I phoned home before I locked up, but there was no reply. Perhaps it's just that he's forgotten, but that's very unusual. The last bus comes from Oxford, and it's always late, so Uncle Lam makes a point of picking me up once the shop closes."

Neal felt that she seemed tense. He wondered aloud if the incident they'd witnessed the previous night was still worrying her.

She smiled apologetically. "Oh, Neal, I'm sorry, but I really think I must have let my imagination run away with me. Mrs Vernon was back in the shop this morning, and I mentioned it to her." She giggled self-consciously. "Not about our late-night vigil, of course. But about the man in the van. To my relief, Sylvie shrugged it away. She passed it off as an arrangement her husband must have made and added sniffily that he never bothered to tell her anything anyway."

Neal wasn't convinced. "I'm surprised by her lack of concern," he commented.

Jill lowered her voice, despite there being only the two of them in the car. "The Vernons' marriage isn't a particularly happy one," she replied. "Sylvie's lovely, and I get on well with her. But Maurice Vernon's a hard-headed businessman. He can be quite overbearing, and I'm not too keen on him."

Neal thought she might have said more, but in the next moment they forgot all about the Vernons. Neal had turned off the main road, and the twisting lane began its descent towards Briar Hedge and its handful of neighbouring cottages. That was when they saw the smoke, thick and black, spiralling towards the darkening sky.

Jill stared in utter disbelief. "But that -? It *can't* be -!"

"The summerhouse!" Neal exclaimed. He'd quickly picked out the orange glare of the flames, could see that the fire was some distance removed from the cottage itself. But if it took hold, it wouldn't be long before the whole lot went up.

He trod on the accelerator, and they plummeted down the hill, squirting gravel in all directions as Neal braked to a halt in front of the cottage.

Jill had turned pale, fidgeting in her seat, and almost before the car had stopped, she'd scrambled out of the passenger door and across to the side gate. Neal was quickly after her, intent on preventing her from getting too close to the blaze. He had the presence of mind to notice the absence of Wilkie's Land Rover.

Sirens wailed in the distance, and he presumed a neighbour must have alerted the fire brigade. Jill had come to an abrupt halt on the back lawn and, momentarily distracted, he'd clattered into her before he could stop, flinging his arms around her to save her from being knocked flat.

She scarcely seemed to notice, waving an unsteady hand in the direction of the summerhouse. The hungry flames had almost entirely consumed the flimsy wooden structure, and Wilkie's shelves of books and memorabilia were no more than piles of searing ash. But Jill's bewildered gaze was fastened on the chair behind her uncle's desk. In it was slumped the body of a man: a human torch, ravaged by the inferno.

Neal witnessed the dumb horror on her face before her voice ripped out in a helpless cry. "Oh, dear God – it's Uncle Lam!"

Suddenly, she'd torn herself from his grasp, lurching towards the burning summerhouse. His flailing fingers snatched at her shoulders, missed, fought for a stronger grip and finally succeeded in hauling her back.

"Jill – no! It's too late."

He hardly recognised the face she turned towards him, her pale, pleasant features a blotched mask of unbridled fury. Beyond them, the windowpane cracked and exploded into fragments. Neal's split-second hesitation gave her the opportunity to once more squirm away from him. As she screamed her uncle's name, he grabbed hold of her, hauled her back and swung her around to face him.

"You can't go any closer, Jill. It's not safe."

Her response was to fight him. He'd heard such abuse before, familiar with every word, but coming from her dainty mouth, each epithet shocked him. She fought him with her hands and fingernails, clawing at his face. He was appalled by her fury, such a quiet, frail, gentle girl, and he needed every ounce of his strength to contain her, hold on to her, because all the while she was battling to escape.

The only respite was that he'd pulled her round to face him, so that she couldn't see the blackened body or be blinded by the swirling flakes of ash. Finally, sensing she'd reached the end of her strength, he hustled her back towards the side gate in a slow, ungainly waltz, relieved to hear the thump of feet on the driveway, as the fire engine drew up and the crew spilled out and started the process of dousing the flames, before the fire could spread to the cottage.

As water gushed over the wreckage of the summerhouse, Neal coaxed Jill back round to the front of the cottage, speaking gently, trying to reason with her and calm her down.

He realised that the body might not be that of Lambert Wilkie, despite Jill's obvious distress. After all, Wilkie's Land Rover had gone. But what if someone else had taken it? He didn't want to tax Jill with that possibility, neither could he be confident that the body wasn't Wilkie's.

Neal said nothing of this to her, but she seemed to sense it in his hesitation, the uncertainty in his voice, for suddenly she was a tigress again, cavorting in his grasp; and as he struggled to restrain her, all the fight went out of her just as quickly, and she collapsed, sobbing, against him. He half-dragged her across the driveway to be met by Tomkins.

The sergeant had parked his Hillman behind the fire engine, and beyond it a constable was keeping the small crowd of onlookers at bay. Neal presumed they were neighbours from farther down the lane, but he noticed Bill Crannock there, looking solemn, and next to him an elegant-looking woman, who'd squeezed through to the front with an air of purpose.

Seeing Jill, she stepped forward. Tomkins moved across to prevent her progressing any further, but she swept past, ignoring his officious protest.

She was a tall, striking woman in her thirties, stylishly turned-out in a beige two-piece suit and matching pumps. Inquisitive brown eyes sparkled beneath a helmet of blonde hair, and she greeted Neal with a dazzling smile, as she held out her arms to receive the distraught girl.

"Please, allow me, Mr -?"

"Gallian."

"Jill, my dear. It's Sylvie."

Her face blotched with weeping, Jill unwound herself from Neal and stepped meekly into the woman's embrace. They had the appearance of mother and daughter: Jill slight, girlish and rumpled, Sylvie tall, reassuring and in full control.

She smiled again at Neal's confusion. "Sylvie Vernon, Mr Gallian. My husband owns the wine shop where Jill works."

"Jill told me," he replied. "Are you happy to – well, look after her?"

"I'll take her back with me," Sylvie Vernon confirmed. "She'll be in good hands, I assure you. I'll put her up for the night." She nodded in the direction of the cottage, from behind which smoke wriggled away into the night sky. "Do you know?" She lowered her voice to a hushed whisper, as she clutched the sobbing girl to her chest. "Is the body the colonel's?"

"No way of telling," he whispered back. "The body of a man, anyway." He didn't say anything about the Land Rover. Its absence opened a whole can of worms. What if the person who'd started the fire had taken it? The fire certainly hadn't started itself, and he couldn't believe Wilkie might have set it off accidentally without having been able to make his escape.

Tomkins rumbled over to join them. Neal had been conscious of him in private conversation with the fire chief at the side gate. He now fixed Neal with a suspicious glance. "I take it yourself and Miss Westmacott were first to arrive at the scene?" he inquired.

Sylvie Vernon cut in quickly. "As you can see, Sergeant, Miss Westmacott's in no fit state to speak to you now."

"I'm aware of that, madam." Tomkins' voice betrayed a hint of asperity.

"I'm taking her home with me," Sylvie swept on. "Perhaps you'd call round to The Leylands in the morning and put your questions to her then. But not tonight."

Neal had to suppress a smile. Sylvie's imperious tone took no prisoners. He felt that, even though she had a good command of English, she spoke with a slight accent. He guessed she might be French.

Tomkins had the good sense to delay comment until Sylvie, with a vacantly staring Jill on her arm, had walked away to where, presumably, she'd left her car.

"Might take longer than that to identify the body," Tomkins muttered darkly, as he watched them go. "Fire chief tells me the poor blighter's burnt to a crisp."

Bill Crannock joined them, with an impassive nod at Neal. "Your constable's giving nothing away," he murmured. "What's up, Tommo?"

"Body in the summerhouse," Tomkins droned. "Place is burned to the ground."

"Not the colonel, is it?" Crannock sounded anxious.

"Too early to say."

"Colonel Wilkie's Land Rover's gone," Neal put in. He watched for Crannock's reaction. To his surprise, he looked relieved; and Neal felt confused. He couldn't make up his mind about Bill Crannock.

"Might not be the colonel, then," Crannock commented. "But if not, who can it be?"

Neal was puzzled by Crannock's concern. However, whether they were mates or not, there was no sympathy from Tomkins.

"It'll take a while to sort that out," he murmured glumly, as if the weight of the world was on his shoulders. He switched Neal an unfavourable glance. "S'pose I'd better get on the blower to your lot, and they can send some confounded CID whizz-kid down to have a rummage through what's left of the summerhouse." He grinned cynically. "That'll muck up somebody's smart suit."

Tomkins barked at his constable to send the few remaining onlookers on their way. Crannock took the hint to leave too, and the sergeant walked Neal over to his car.

"The mercy is the fire didn't spread to the house," he said. "That thatch must be tinder-dry. Right, I'd better get back round and find out what else the fire chief's got to report. I'm -er, presuming the place was well ablaze when you arrived back here with Miss Westmacott?"

Tomkins' tone held a hint of suspicion, which Neal ignored. "I was passing through Braxbury and stopped at the bus stop to offer Miss Westmacott a lift. Her uncle had been supposed to pick her up from the shop half-an-hour earlier."

The sergeant grinned lewdly. "Very public-spirited of you, I'm sure," he mumbled and ambled across to the side gate.

An ambulance arrived as Neal squeezed his car past the fire engine into the lane. He very much feared that they might be carrying away the mortal remains of Colonel Lambert Wilkie.

14

On his return to Oxford, he made the decision to take the car across to France the next day and make inquiries in Valleronde, the town where Roger had last been seen nineteen years previously. He didn't think there was anything to be gained in Braxbury, at least not for a while. He wouldn't get much change from Crannock and had no lead as to where Jacko Manning might have gone; although the signs were that he hadn't gone willingly.

Neal wondered if he should turn that over to the police. But Tomkins, he was sure, would be of little help, and even though there was a DCI at Oxford, Don Pilling, whom he respected, he didn't think he'd be greatly interested. Manning was a small-time villain, and whether or not he really was going straight, his disappearance would be low on the list of priorities.

So, it would have to be Valleronde. He'd learned from Wilkie that a local resistance man had led Roger's party up to Chateau Garay. Provided the man was still alive, Neal intended to track him down and see if he could obtain any new leads.

He booked a berth on the afternoon ferry from Southampton the following day. Before starting out the next morning, he touched base with Tomkins. The sergeant was less than thrilled to hear from him and informed him with morbid glee that the body in the summerhouse still hadn't been identified. He hadn't yet had the chance to interview Jill Westmacott and made it sound as if that was Neal's fault. Neal grinned: he guessed Sylvie Vernon was playing hard to get.

Neal thought about phoning Jill at the Vernons'. But with no news regarding her uncle, he felt awkward about what to say. Examining his face in the mirror as he shaved, he saw that Jill had left her mark on him. He guessed she might feel embarrassed about that but, for his own part, bore no ill will. He decided it'd be best if he saw her on his return, because he didn't intend staying long in Valleronde. The visit would stir painful memories. Neal had never once been there in the whole nineteen years since Roger's disappearance. In the early days, his father had forbidden it, bound by his shame and torment; and in recent years, Neal had stayed away in deference to him.

He felt sorry for Jill, for if the body turned out to be Wilkie's, he knew she'd be devastated. And yet he recognised a certain resilience in her. She was rather shy and withdrawn, qualities with which he could identify. But she was no shrinking violet: the scratches on his cheeks and neck bore testimony to that.

And the thought of Jill brought back another memory.

A memory of a girl he'd tried his best to protect, who'd privately named him her 'gallant Gallian'.

*

"I can't let this go on."

The bruise under her eye, raw purple on her pale but pleasant face.

"I hoped I could keep it from you," Helen whispered.

Had she? It couldn't have been more obvious, as obvious as the name of the man who'd caused it.

So, what had motivated Neal? Looking back, he wondered if it might have been her artifice. For she looked so forlorn, so vulnerable and without a friend.

No. Not without…

"You're the only friend I have, Neal."

"Helen – I can't let this go on."

But he had. She'd begged him to say nothing to Clyde, even while admitting that it had happened before. The time came, finally, when he could stand it no longer: her hurt, her pain, her dejection. He overruled her: he would speak to Clyde.

But for another reason, they both knew he wouldn't.

And he didn't.

"You're the only friend I have, Neal. My gallant Gallian. My knight in shining armour."

Oh, how he detested the clichés, the platitudes now. And yet how incapable had he been then of seeing them as just that.

Because he'd held her then. She'd collapsed, then, into his not-by-any-means reluctant embrace. They'd kissed.

And there'd been the subsequent occasions when they'd kissed. Neal was old-fashioned, imbued with a code of honour: it was the way he'd been taught to live. But Helen had been hurt, and he couldn't stand for that; and she'd been hurt again, again. She needed to be comforted, needed a friend she could believe in.

They'd kissed; and kissed again.

Moved on from kissing…

"I can't let this go on."
But he had. And suddenly Clyde was no longer there.

*

He'd lain in his hospital bed in a side ward, wrapped in his guilt and shame. The wounds were healing; somehow, he'd almost forgotten them.

And still she hadn't come to see him: that hurt most of all.

One day, he awoke from a troubled doze, his shoulder hurting like fury despite the surgery and the painkillers. He opened his eyes, and she was standing sullenly beside his bed. He wondered for a second if he was caught up in a bad dream, for he'd never seen her glowering like this; or glowering at all.

"Helen – I -. Oh, Helen, I'm sorry, so sorry. Please, please sit down."

But she wouldn't sit. She wasn't going to stay. She'd brought no grapes, no flowers. No greeting.

"You let him down, Neal." Her voice was muffled in anger. Hers? It sounded like the voice of a stranger. "You called yourself his friend. You could have saved him. Why did he have to die, Neal? Why did you let him die? It was down to you. It's all *your* fault."

She turned and left, slamming the door behind her. He lay there and stared after her for what seemed like hours, immobilised with shock, devastated with *his* hurt, *his* pain.

His guilt.

"Why did you let him die?"

He thought now of Jill's fury, Jill fighting him, Jill lashing out with blow upon blow in her grief, her bewilderment.

They'd been nothing compared to the debilitating blows Helen had dealt him. Helen, who'd not laid a finger upon him.

He heard, later, that she'd left Oxford, moved up to her sister's in Edinburgh. He wangled the address out of Tom Wrightson and wrote to her, a long letter shouldering the blame, outlining his regrets, asking her forgiveness.

He received no reply, wrote again, leaving a telephone number.

Two years on, and he'd heard nothing. Helen Holt had comprehensively walked out of his life.

"Why didn't you save him?"

Because he knew he could have done so, would have done. But he'd reacted too slowly, too late…

And all that he had left now were those two morose and unforgiving bedfellows.

Guilt. And shame.

15

The ferry docked at Cherbourg late that evening, and Neal drove fifty kilometres inland to the town of Valleronde. Here he found a *pension* in the tangle of streets beyond the square and, after a few hours' fitful sleep and a light breakfast, went out to explore the town.

It seemed to be thriving, the bars and bistros enjoying a brisk trade with tourists, tables with bright parasols spilling out on to the cobbled walkways, the little gift shops quaint and enticing, replete with their tacky souvenirs.

The church of St Sauveur stood in the centre of the town, and behind it lay the communal gardens bursting with floral displays around the tall, imposing statue of Alain Brissart, Comte de Valleronde, who, Neal gathered, was the town's local hero.

He made his way into the church. It was plainly furnished, the pews, altar, the stations of the cross around the grey walls all hewn from the same dark, age-defying wood. He slipped into a pew, sat for a while, absorbing the peace, and bowed his head.

He doubted the interior would have changed at all since Roger's time and wondered if his brother might have come here, sat in one of these pews and reflected on what had been, what might be to come. Not long before he'd arrived in Valleronde, Roger would have learned of the death of his friend Philip Norreys, killed in the D-Day landings. That would have been a crushing blow to him, but Roger, a thoughtful, private man, would hardly have confided his feelings to anyone else. He might well have sat here and prayed, poured out the turmoil in his heart to the listening God.

Roger had gone bravely to war. His country, his father, would have demanded it, but from the few letters he'd sent home, Neal had always believed he'd not gone with a whole heart. With Philip's death – Philip, who'd been like a brother to him, the boys inseparable since they'd known one another at boarding school – might not Roger have seen the hopelessness, the pointlessness of war, its indiscriminate slaughter, its impromptu shutting-off of human lives, the diabolical misery it brought?

Might such dark thoughts have helped tip the scales?

There was no time to reflect further on the matter, for suddenly Neal was aware of voices and movement. The voices were loud, twangy and American, and he looked around as a group of nine or ten people bundled into the church, the women in shades, sun hats and billowing skirts, the men in jazzy shirts, panama hats clutched respectfully to their chests. They were led by a guide, fat, crafty and wearing a perpetual fawning smile, trying to look smart in a linen suit, white shirt and blue cravat.

He was speaking to the party in good English, explaining the significance of the church, its crypt the last resting-place of the gallant Comte, whose residence had been the imposing Chateau Garay on the hill, where he, Pierre, would next take them. Neal rose from his pew and tagged along behind them.

They made their way down a narrow flight of stone steps in the far corner of the church, the girth of several of the party ensuring that progress was slow. The crypt was dim, cool and musty. Cameras flashed, although all Neal could make out were the stark outlines of half-a-dozen stone tombs.

Pierre explained that here lay the Comte, Alain Brissart, the saviour of Valleronde, along with his wife and a few descendants. He would tell them more once they'd reached the chateau, including the reasons why the inhabitants of Valleronde were eternally grateful to their noble hero.

The tourists crowded around the tomb, but there was really nothing to see. Pierre fielded a couple of inane questions and, with a sly wink at Neal, trundled past him and led the party back up into the main body of the church. The Americans filed after him obediently, and Neal brought up the rear, content to wander several yards behind the rest, who were anyway enthusing among themselves about this 'bee-ootiful little village'.

They trawled up the hill towards the Chateau Garay. Red-bricked and imposing, its black turrets fencing at the cloudless sky, Pierre explained that the chateau had been the home of Brissart and his descendants until the line had died out in the late 1800s, whereafter it had been bought by a family of rich Jewish bankers. It was now held in trust, a showpiece which was the jewel in Valleronde's crown.

As they left the town below them, several of the group beginning to labour and bemoan "this awful steep climb", Neal tracked the route Roger and his reconnaissance party must have taken. To his left lay a patch of woodland, which skirted the chateau's grounds before falling away into open countryside. He recalled Wilkie telling him that the resistance man had led the group up through the woods to emerge on to a road just below the main gates. Had anyone been lying in wait, the woodland would have provided adequate cover for Roger and his men.

Pierre proudly led his charges through the dining room of the early Renaissance chateau into the Great Hall, showing off the fluted pilasters round the doors and windows, the hand-carved furniture and *chinoiserie* murals, as well as the paintings and porcelain collections of the current owners, to the accompaniment of stunned exclamations and merrily clicking cameras.

As they gathered around the vast open fireplace, he recounted the tale of the noble Comte de Valleronde.

Alain Brissart had been a dashing young soldier in the King's Guard. He stood to inherit the chateau and title from his uncle Philippe, who'd brought him up from a boy. However, an older cousin, Henri de Gonfleur, whom Alain distrusted, lived nearby and was trying hard to worm his way into his uncle's affections.

Philippe was very old and ill and not expected to last much longer. Alain would have wished to be with him in those last days, but his duty as a musketeer was to the king, and he was called away. It was reported that he'd met his end in the Siege of La Rochelle. The information was false, and it was suspected that de Gonfleur had been instrumental in spreading the rumour.

However, the news was a death blow to Philippe, who'd loved Alain dearly and treated him as a son. Once the old Comte had passed away, de Gonfleur usurped his young cousin and established himself in his uncle's place as master of Valleronde.

The little town was soon in his thrall. De Gonfleur and his band of hangers-on bled the merchants dry by taking their goods and never paying their bills. No woman was safe from them, and anyone who tried to stand in their way was summarily removed. The inhabitants lived in fear, the chateau became notorious for its riotous orgies, and the prayers of the faithful seemed to have fallen on deaf ears.

Until the day Alain Brissart unexpectedly returned. He was intercepted on his way back to the chateau by a farmer, Gilles Vaupin, who'd always been loyal to Philippe. He explained to Alain what had happened and, in tears, recounted how his own beloved daughter had been ill-used.

Alain, normally a mild-mannered young man, flew into a towering rage. He had the sense to recognise, however, that if he confronted de Gonfleur alone, he would be set upon by the brutes his cousin kept as retainers. So, he bided his time at Vaupin's farm, instructing the noble Gilles to secretly gather every man who could use a sword, staff or musket to meet together at the farm under cover of darkness.

One night, backed by two dozen fighting men, Alain Brissart rode boldly into the Chateau Garay and burst into the dining room. All who'd been carousing there, except for a few who'd already drunk themselves into a stupor, turned tail and fled. Alain ordered his men to rescue their womenfolk and deal with any of de Gonfleur's retinue who resisted. His sword drawn, Alain chased his cousin into the Great Hall and challenged him to a duel.

De Gonfleur's response was to hide behind three armed lackeys, who advanced towards Brissart.

Alain engaged with them. He was a nimble, gifted swordsman and took little time to disable them. He challenged de Gonfleur again but, as he'd guessed, the man was an abject coward. He surrendered immediately and vowed to make reparation for all the misery he'd caused. Once that had been done, he was banished to Italy and was never heard of again.

Alain Brissart took up his rightful place as Comte de Valleronde, married Gilles Vaupin's daughter and, at his own expense, rebuilt the town, which soon began to thrive again. For over fifty years, he dealt justly and compassionately with his tenants, brought stability to the region and was greatly revered by all.

"Sadly, Brissart's line died out towards the end of the last century," Pierre told his party. He went on to say that the chateau had been purchased in the 1920s by a Jewish banker named Julius Markstein who, to find favour with the locals, had changed his name to Jules Marichaux. He was greatly interested in art and had built up a magnificent collection by the time of the Occupation. In 1940, he and his wife were taken away by the Nazis to perish in a concentration camp. The chateau became the German regional HQ, and its commandant, Colonel von Rinksdorf, took charge of Marichaux's art treasures as well as others which he'd purloined from various sources as he'd made his way across France. Von Rinksdorf had been curator of a Berlin art museum before the war and built up a peerless collection during his time at the Chateau Garay.

Had he left them behind after the town was liberated? one of the tourists wanted to know.

Pierre chuckled nastily. "The commandant left in a hurry," he replied. "He had one of those big German staff cars and bundled as much as he could into it. He fled but, sadly for him, didn't get far. He was tracked down and hung after the war. But before that, he made a good fist of getting rid of what he could. As a former curator, he'd built up a list of contacts, and much of poor old Marichaux's collection ended up in the sticky hands of private collectors. So, our von Rinksdorf died a rich man, if it's any consolation." He laughed harshly, a loud guffaw. "But probably not much to him!"

Once the guided tour was over and the Americans had left to straggle back down to the town, Neal drew Pierre aside. The man was in high spirits, evidenced by the number of fifty-franc notes he was carefully folding into his wallet, and all attention as he palmed the note Neal held out to him.

"I was very interested in hearing what you had to say about the Germans abandoning the chateau," Neal said. "You see, my brother was among those who liberated Valleronde in 1944 and was involved in reclaiming this chateau. Apparently, one of the resistance men led my brother's detachment up through the woods. I wondered if you might have some idea who that could have been?"

Pierre laughed uproariously. "Why, that could only have been my lifelong friend and partner in crime, Armand Delacourt. We fought each other at school, fought over the girls as young men and fought together in the resistance! Armand would have been eager to look around the chateau himself at the earliest opportunity. You see, he worked with his father in the antiques business before the war. As soon as the filthy Boche arrived, the Delacourts shut up shop and stowed away anything of value in the church crypt. Old Father Simon knew all about it, of course. Very partial to a fine Armagnac, that one.

"However, once Armand got up here with the British soldiers, he found little of any worth. Our gutless von Rinksdorf had had much of it away."

"Is Delacourt still around?" Neal asked.

"Ha! Indeed, *mon ami*. Large as life and thriving. The old man is long dead, of course, but they reopened the shop after the war, and through much hard work built up the business again. He has a number of rich clients in Europe and America. You'll find his shop in the square. I'm sure he'll be glad to oblige you – provided, naturally, that you don't interrupt a sale."

16

Neal walked back down to the cobbled square, passing the majestic Hotel de la Paix, its walls gleaming with recent paint, glossy red shutters flung open at the windows and a profusion of plants trailing from the bright green window boxes.

Beyond the humming bars, bistros and gift shops, as if trying to set itself apart, stood Armand Delacourt's antique shop, its air of prosperity underlined by the prices of the items displayed in its bay window. Neal went in, his arrival announced by the prim 'ping' of the doorbell. The two people in the shop looked up before returning to their discussion, the man according Neal a brief nod and small smile to acknowledge his presence.

Neal took the opportunity to look around: all manner of antiques, each clearly priced and labelled in a precise, italic hand with a concise description of their provenance. Everything was neatly, perhaps obsessively arranged, the walkways uncluttered, with the more delicate wares, such as porcelain and cutlery, housed in glass cabinets.

Neal presumed the man was Delacourt. He was fawning over an elderly, white-haired, bejewelled matron, who was haughtily resisting his efforts to sell her a gilt ormolu clock. From the far side of one of the cabinets, Neal studied the man.

He was suave and silver-haired, probably in his late fifties. He wore a well-cut grey suit which sought to disguise his paunch, gold cuff links, red bow tie and highly polished black shoes. His manner was unctuous, bordering on oily, and Neal's first impression was that he didn't like him. He found it difficult to imagine Delacourt as a doughty resistance fighter; but then, neither could he envisage the portly Pierre in the same way. The war had, after all, been over for eighteen years. They'd have been different men, younger, leaner, bent on survival and the liberation of their little town.

Finally, the woman gave in, and they agreed a price. Neal gathered that the duel had ended in victory for Delacourt, for he was effusive and painstakingly attentive as he parcelled up the purchase, whereas the woman counted out several one-hundred-franc notes from her handbag, slapping one after the other down on the counter with an air of regret. Delacourt thanked her, placed the purchase lovingly in her grasp, escorted her to the door and slavishly bowed her out. Closing the door with unnecessary care, he turned, nodding towards the glass cabinet, the contents of which Neal had pretended to be studying.

"Good afternoon, *m'sieu*. How may I be of service?"

"Armand Delacourt?"

"But of course."

"My name is Neal Gallian." Neal looked directly at Delacourt as he gave his name, wondering if he might get some reaction. He wasn't disappointed, for the antiques dealer appeared momentarily taken aback.

He recovered quickly. "Ah, yes. Perhaps you'd care to take a seat, *m'sieu*?"

He indicated a small desk towards the rear of the shop, on which stood a tray containing cups, saucers and a jug of coffee on a hotplate. There was a chair either side of the desk, and Delacourt installed himself in the one facing the street door, while offering Neal the other. He poured coffee into both cups, took a sip from his and set it back in the saucer, before turning a face of polite inquiry towards his visitor.

"Gallian, you say?"

"I believe the name may sound familiar?"

"Oh, but it does. I can place it exactly – from the time of Valleronde's glorious liberation. Clearly you are a relative?"

"Roger is my elder brother."

"I see. Please – I must allow you to enlighten me further."

Delacourt settled comfortably in his chair, hands folded in his lap and head cocked in readiness to hear what Neal had to say.

Neal told his story. "The tour guide at the Chateau Garay – Pierre?"

Armand Delacourt smiled, displaying perfect teeth which Neal suspected weren't his own. "Ah, yes. My old and dear friend Pierre Audoin – we served together in the resistance during the war."

"I'd gathered as much. It was you who took the reconnaissance party up through the woods to the chateau?"

"That's true, M'sieu Gallian. And to this day, I find myself worrying over your brother's disappearance. My own theory is that somehow he met with an ambush in his pursuit of the sniper, that he was killed, and his body taken away?" He shrugged, spreading his hands in a helpless gesture. "Who knows? But I assume nothing more was heard of him?"

"Nothing."

"Then you feel the conclusion the authorities reached must be the correct one?"

"That Roger descrted? It's the theory everyone seems to have accepted."

"But you don't?" Delacourt was looking sceptical. "All this happened nearly twenty years ago, M'sieu Gallian. I'm a little surprised that it's only now that you're looking into it."

For a moment, Neal was lost for words. Of course, they – he and his father – should have stirred themselves long ago. Delacourt's reprimand was deserved.

"My father wouldn't hear of it," he replied lamely. "He was a proud man, an ex-army major. All the reports reached the same conclusion, and he had to accept them. He tried to blot the memory of Roger out of his life. I don't think he ever succeeded, but he forced himself to accept those conclusions."

"And now?"

"Father died three years ago." *And I've just come back to life, kick-started myself into trying to do something about it.*

Neal didn't put those thoughts into words, neither was he about to tell Delacourt of the events of the last few days, how Jacko Manning's chance conversation had led him here. To be fair, Delacourt didn't pursue it, made no allusion as to how it had taken three years for Neal to lurch into action.

"I know it happened a long time ago," he went on. "Perhaps too long to matter now. But you see, *m'sieu,* the brother I knew and looked up to was no coward, no deserter. I came here to ask if you might know anyone who belonged to a neighbouring resistance group. If Roger was wounded in going after the sniper, might someone have found him, tended to him, set him back on his feet again?"

He knew he was snatching at straws, and even though Delacourt was looking sympathetic, he was already shaking his head.

"If that had been the case," he said, "I'm certain that I, or one of my compatriots, would have heard. But the authorities at the time – your brother's commanding officer, I believe – left no stone unturned. No-one knew anything. Or if they did," he added darkly, "they weren't telling."

Neal might have taken umbrage, because he understood Delacourt to be suggesting that Roger might have bribed someone to help him reach Spain or one of the French ports on the west coast. But he kept his irritation in check: there was no point in angering the antiques dealer, who'd been his last hope.

And yet, he felt there had to be *something:* Stoker's death, Manning's abduction, the body – Wilkie's? – in the charred remains of the summerhouse at Briar Hedge. He was determined to keep on probing, but for today he'd gone far enough. He wasn't sold on Delacourt but believed the man had been as helpful as he could. He changed tack and, looking around, remarked that the business seemed to be doing well.

Delacourt nodded judiciously. "Things have improved greatly in these last years. It was not so for some time after the war."

"Pierre told me the Germans had left very little at the chateau."

The antiques dealer laughed bitterly. "Ha! My poor father was distraught – you should have seen him! That swine von Rinksdorf only left what he couldn't cram into that oversized staff car – and that wasn't much, I can tell you. Still, the bastard got what was coming to him."

He glanced past Neal, his attention suddenly gripped. "Ah, *m'sieu!* It seems I have another visitor." He shoved back his chair and scrambled to his feet. "By all that is wonderful, fortune is indeed smiling upon me today."

Neal stood and turned as he heard the 'ping' of the doorbell, followed by the click of a woman's heels. He smelt the delicate waft of expensive perfume. If the woman happened to be attractive, he found himself sincerely hoping that she wouldn't turn out to be Delacourt's wife or lady friend, although the man had swept her into a fond embrace and was eagerly applying the traditional Gallic greeting of multiple kisses.

So, probably not his wife, but certainly, from Neal's first brief glimpse, attractive and easily a head taller than Delacourt. She was elegantly turned out in a white and turquoise-striped summer frock and white sandals. Neal noticed, beneath her white, wide-brimmed hat, a moue of revulsion as her ardent admirer cavorted around her, his hands everywhere.

And then he froze in astonishment as his eyes met hers, and a smile of both welcome and relief lit up her face. For Delacourt's winsome visitor was none other than the woman Neal had met at Briar Hedge two nights previously.

Sylvie Vernon.

17

"Good afternoon, Mrs Vernon."

"Ah, Mr Gallian. What a pleasant surprise."

Sylvie's eyes gleamed mischievously beneath the brim of her hat, amused that her sudden appearance had rocked him, for Neal was certain his face was testimony to that.

Delacourt was similarly taken aback. "Then you -er, you know one another? A strange coincidence, is it not?"

He sounded a little put out, and Neal didn't mind that. But what really puzzled him was what Sylvie Vernon was doing there in Valleronde. Only two nights ago she'd been in Braxbury comforting Jill Westmacott. Jill had been devastated, probably in shock. Why hadn't Sylvie remained with her?

"Mr Gallian and I have a mutual friend in Braxbury." Sylvie's reply was offhand, but Delacourt was going to have to make do with it.

Neal, however, was determined to get a straight answer to his question.

"How's Jill?" he asked. "Is she well enough to be left alone?"

He guessed she'd noticed his concern, for she approached him, sweeping past Delacourt, and laid a placatory hand on his arm, her touch both reassuring and sensual.

"Ah, of course, you won't have heard. The sergeant informed us yesterday morning – the body is not that of Colonel Wilkie. At present they're not sure whose, but it's certainly not his."

Neal blew out his cheeks. "What a relief for Jill!"

"Indeed," Sylvie agreed with a smile. "I offered to stay, but she's gone back home in the hope that her uncle will make contact. There's been no sign of him, and the police are keen to track him down."

If the body wasn't Wilkie's, and he couldn't be found, Neal was sure they'd want to do that and have some searching questions for him. But he said nothing, in fact wasn't given the chance, for Delacourt had taken advantage of his hesitation to remind them that he was present, clearing his throat diplomatically.

He was looking puzzled, as well he might, and Sylvie decided at last to put him out of his misery. She was smiling as she did so, and Neal felt sure she was savouring the man's confusion.

"There was a fire in Braxbury, Armand," she explained. "Tragically, a man died. Mr Gallian here, and my young friend Jill Westmacott, were first to arrive on the scene but sadly unable to help him. I'll tell you more later."

The antiques dealer's face lit up. In Neal's opinion, he'd been standing far too close to Sylvie and took the opportunity to place an arm around her waist. "Then I am to see you again later?" Colour had risen to his cheeks, and his excited expression gave Neal the impression of a greedy schoolboy who'd just received the promise of a food hamper. "This is indeed my lucky day. Will you do me the honour of dining with me this evening, then, *ma chérie*? I recall time was against us on your last visit."

"I'm afraid it was, Armand." From his cosy position, Delacourt was unable to see, once again, her pout of distaste. It was clear Sylvie wished time might have been the issue again.

"You are staying in the square as usual?"

"At La Paix, yes."

"Then we shall dine there. Maurice too, if he's free?" Delacourt left the sentence hanging, indicating that in his opinion three would be a crowd.

"Oh, Maurice will be busy wheeling and dealing," she threw back scornfully. She smiled at Neal. "My husband," she explained. "He's here on a wine-buying trip, and I am, as always on such occasions, the grass widow." She chuckled lightly. "Perhaps the wine widow, more appropriately. We shall travel back together, just to be able to say we've spoken to one another."

She sounded weary, and Neal recalled Jill telling him that the Vernons didn't exactly hit it off. It made him wonder if Maurice Vernon should see an optician. For his wife was an attractive woman, tall, blonde and willowy, with a lively sense of humour. Certainly, Delacourt was smitten.

In fact, he found Delacourt disgusting: typical of an older man besotted with a younger woman. The antiques dealer's eyes bulged lustfully, and there was a sheen of perspiration on his plump face, as he bobbed energetically around her.

Sylvie had had enough. "I must go now, Armand. I wish to look into Garnier's before they close."

"But of course, *ma chérie*. Until this evening, then, at La Paix. Let us say seven-thirty?"

"Delighted." She reached down and pointedly uncoiled Delacourt's arm from around her waist, before turning to go.

Neal decided to leave at the same time, although where Delacourt was concerned, he'd been surplus to requirements for a while.

The antiques dealer shook his hand, seized the opportunity to once more embrace and kiss Sylvie and proceeded to bow her out of the shop. As he walked beside her across the square, Neal sensed Delacourt watching from the shop doorway, his gaze rivetted to the practised sway of her hips. He noticed several other admiring glances; and it didn't surprise him that his fair companion wasn't in the least embarrassed.

As they walked, he remarked upon the coincidence that Sylvie had originally come from Valleronde.

"Not Valleronde exactly," she replied with an engaging smile. "My parents have a farm about twenty kilometres away, near Beaurallier. They're both getting on in years, but my father stubbornly refuses to retire – he's farmed all his life, so I suppose I can understand his feelings. Maurice comes over here a lot in the course of his work, and it gives me the chance to regularly check up on them." The smile was wicked now. "A dutiful daughter, am I not? But what exactly brings you here, Neal?"

It wasn't lost on him that she'd used his Christian name: she must have learned it from Jill and clearly wasn't one to stand on ceremony. He gave a brief account of Roger's disappearance and the reason for his visit to Delacourt. She listened attentively, but Neal couldn't shake off the impression that she already knew about it.

"Ah, yes, I believe Jill mentioned it." She flashed him a teasing glance from beneath her fringe. "You are, I think – how shall I put it? – on friendly terms with Jill."

He tried to answer blandly, but his unease was plain and drew another wicked smile from her.

"Er, just friends," he said.

"Of course."

He could tell she understood the situation and was relieved that she had the grace not to stare too obviously at his reddening face. He clumsily changed tack. "Er, your husband – you say he comes over here regularly?"

"As clockwork." Sylvie sounded bored. "He buys from several vineyards in the region. He used to work in one near here, when he was learning the trade. In fact, that's how we met." The smile had faded.

Neal decided not to pursue the subject of Maurice Vernon and changed it again. "You've known Monsieur Delacourt for some time?"

She raised her eyebrows sardonically. "For longer than I can remember – as he never tires of reminding me. He's a friend of my father's."

"He certainly seems fond of you."

If he'd been hoping to pay Sylvie back with some embarrassment, he failed miserably. However, she hadn't smiled for a little while now.

"Too much, unfortunately," she sighed. "One day, Maurice may notice. Although I'm not counting on it."

They'd arrived outside a boutique at the far side of the square. "Here's another reason for revisiting Valleronde," Sylvie announced. "I'm a good customer." A sales assistant stood holding open the door, smiling at her in welcome.

"I'm sure we shall bump into one another again, Neal," Sylvie went on. She leaned forward, steadying herself against him as she stumbled in her heels, and kissed him lightly on each cheek. He didn't think it entirely a coincidence that her breast brushed his arm as she withdrew.

Then she was gone, sashaying into the shop and cheerfully returning the assistant's effusive greeting. She bequeathed another waft of perfume in her wake.

Neal headed back to his *pension*, wondering on coincidences and where they might lead. He wasn't to know then that there were more to come.

18

Neal knew that, on his budget, there was no question of him dining at the Hotel de la Paix, even if he'd wanted to, and he was happy to leave Sylvie Vernon and Armand Delacourt to it. He returned to his room for a wash and change of shirt, before setting out to find somewhere for a cheap but substantial evening meal.

Behind Valleronde's square lay a maze of narrow streets full of bars and cafés. It was an area off the tourist trail and frequented by the local community. Neal felt more at ease there and, even though he hadn't studied French since his schooldays, he had an aptitude for it and was adept enough to make himself understood and work out the drift of conversations going on around him.

A dinner of steak and *pommes frites* accompanied by a demi-carafe of house red proved very satisfying. Under different circumstances, Neal might have felt reasonably relaxed; but he had far too much on his mind.

There was the whole question of Roger. Here he was, years further on, perhaps years too late, in the town where his brother had last been seen. Where had he gone? Neal had never been particularly hopeful that Delacourt might have been able to add anything, and that had proved to be the case. And yet…

And yet he still felt there was *something*, felt that he might be on the right track. Was he deluding himself, snatching at hope where none was to be found? Only time would tell.

He cast his mind back to Braxbury, the night of the fire, to Jill. He was glad for her, was able to understand the measure of her relief that, after all, the body in the charred ruins of the summerhouse hadn't been that of her uncle. But did she in her turn understand that it begged other questions? For instance, whose body was it? Where was Lambert Wilkie, and what was the reason for his sudden disappearance? The answers to those, once found, might cause her considerable distress. Neal decided to return to England the next day, felt he needed to be on hand for her.

The evening wasn't far advanced, and he decided he'd have a walk through the back streets and maybe call into a bar for a cognac before returning to his *pension*. He rounded off his meal with a coffee, paid up and started to make his way out. He was on the point of stepping out into the street when someone hurried past on the narrow pavement, causing Neal to draw back inside, stare after the man and finally reach the conclusion that his eyes weren't playing tricks.

Bill Crannock.

And the question which immediately followed: *what was he doing in Valleronde?*

Maybe it was a coincidence, but Neal wasn't a great believer in those. He set off in pursuit.

It was clear that Crannock hadn't seen him, for the man had rushed past, was hurrying now and seemed oblivious to his surroundings, his gaze set dead ahead. As he reached the end of the street, he stalked across the road without looking, instantly incurring the wrath of the driver of a 2CV, who had to brake sharply to avoid him. A volley of choice abuse was hurled after him, but Crannock merely glanced back disdainfully at the incandescent driver and went his way.

As he turned his head briefly, Neal caught a glimpse of his expression. If the driver was irate, Crannock was bordering on rage. His mouth was set in an uncompromising scowl, and his eyes burned viciously. Having cursed loudly and freely, the 2CV driver wisely chose to move on. Bill Crannock was a big man, and at that moment looked dangerously mean.

Neal didn't need to follow for long. Halfway down the next street, Crannock disappeared into a bar. There were the obligatory tables out on the pavement and plenty of customers, several of whom were lingering just inside the doorway, chatting and smoking. Fishing a pack of *Gauloises* from his trouser pocket, Neal lit up and hovered on the fringes of the group, from where he had a good view of the bar area.

Crannock stood at the bar, still looking angry. He was next to a smug-looking, thickset man of forty, whose swept-back dark hair gleamed with brilliantine. The man wore a camel-hair coat, and a brown homburg rested on the bar at his elbow.

Camel Hair was puffing at a large cigar and drinking *pastis*. He'd just called for another, which the barman set before his companion. Crannock didn't look appeased, splashing water into the glass and demolishing the drink in two gulps. The man looked on unmoved and lazily signalled for a refill. Crannock treated it with more deference but remained sullen. Camel Hair was speaking, and Neal strained to overhear. The man spoke in English, his voice betraying a London background, his words quietly spoken, but with a latent force.

"Sorry, Bill, but there's no other way. We have to do it again. Darmon's expecting you, so make sure you're ready for tomorrow night's ferry. I can't afford any further delay."

Crannock slammed his glass down on the bar, his face suffused with fury.

"We?" he snarled. "Oh, yes, I like that. It's *me* taking all the risks, chum, while you cruise back over in your flash car, clean as a whistle. And now, a week later, I have to do it all over again. It's hardly my fault that our friend decides to go missing."

The man's voice assumed a hard edge. "I don't give a toss about him – and he's not *my* friend. He's cut out and brought me a lot of grief. *You* brought him into this, Billy boy, so the mess is down to you. You make the pick-up tomorrow and catch the night ferry. I'll see you then. And listen – you'd better not fail me! There's a lot riding on this. More than you might think."

Crannock growled a response, which Neal didn't think was complimentary, and stormed off. His departure was so precipitate, that Neal didn't have time to get out of the way. He turned quickly aside to avoid being recognised, but Crannock was too preoccupied to notice anything, brushing roughly past so that Neal was forced back against the wall.

Camel Hair watched Crannock depart, his face inscrutable. As Neal recovered his balance, he happened to look up, and their eyes met. He offered a careless shrug, which he hoped looked suitably Gallic. The man raised an eyebrow and picked up his drink, turning his back on Neal.

Here was another mystery, and he decided to find out where Crannock was staying. He had every intention of tailing him the next day, as well as returning to England on the night ferry.

He followed Crannock back the way he'd come. The man strode along bad-temperedly, caught up in his own dark thoughts, which made tailing him easy. The route took them across the fiercely illuminated square past the Hotel de la Paix. Neal glimpsed Sylvie Vernon through one of the restaurant windows. Dressed in a sparkling evening gown, she sat across from Delacourt, sleek in his tuxedo and paying her close attention.

Neal chuckled wryly. It didn't surprise him that Sylvie seemed well in control of the situation. He imagined she'd learned how to play the lusting antiques dealer some time ago and would charmingly give him the slip once he was hopelessly drunk.

In the approaching darkness, he managed to lose Crannock in the tangle of streets beyond the square and guessed their accommodations would be of similar status. He was rewarded, however, when he stumbled across a van parked in a side street. The legend on the side read *W. Crannock, Courier, Braxbury, Oxfordshire.* Crannock's lodgings probably lay a short distance ahead.

More to the point, however, the vehicle was a dark green Commer van.

19

Neal breakfasted early the next morning, determined to find out the nature of Crannock's mission and the reason for his anger. He collected his car and found a parking space a little way down the street from the van. He crossed over to a small café, where he could sit outside with a coffee and keep watch.

He didn't have long to wait before Crannock hove into view at the top end of the street. He wouldn't need to come as far down as the café to reach his van, but as a precaution, Neal left his seat and stepped back into the doorway. He watched Crannock get in and manoeuvre out of his parking space. Once he'd driven past the café and turned off at the end of the street, Neal hurried across to the car and set about following him.

He was glad that Crannock wasn't intent on breaking any speed records, cruising along within the limit. Even so, Neal hung well back. There wasn't much traffic, and his quarry's suspicions might be aroused if he spotted a British car on his tail.

Neal had been puzzling over the identity of the man in the camel hair coat, but when, some ten kilometres on, Crannock turned down a minor road signposted *Vignoble Darmon,* he was left in no doubt. Camel Hair had to be Maurice Vernon, and Crannock would be collecting a consignment of wine to take back to Braxbury. Yet surely a missing batch of wine hadn't warranted the aggression shown by Vernon the previous evening? And Crannock's anger had seemed well over the top for the inconvenience of having to make another delivery so soon after the previous one.

Neal wondered if the consignment in question didn't concern wine at all.

A little way down the road, the van turned off into a vineyard. In the distance, workers were busy tending the vines on the sun-dappled slopes: an idyllic scene, but Neal suspected darker business was about to be transacted.

As he drove past the gateway, he saw that Crannock had drawn up outside a large, ugly, red-bricked house with brown shutters, beyond which lay several stone outhouses. He followed the road, which turned sharply left and ran alongside a high drystone wall. He pulled up on to the grass verge, cut the engine and got out.

Neal hoisted himself far enough up the wall to peer over. Bill Crannock was standing by his van and raised a hand in greeting to a short, swarthy, bearded man, who'd emerged from the house. Neal took him to be the vineyard owner, Darmon, whose name he'd heard Vernon mention in the bar the night before.

Crannock's French was gruff and fractured, Darmon's low and guttural. Neither man seemed in particularly good humour, and Neal had no difficulty hearing the many expletives; but the men were standing some distance from the wall, and the rest of their conversation was indistinct.

The argument was fierce, but Crannock stood his ground. Finally, Darmon threw up his hands, swore some more and beckoned him over to one of the outhouses, fishing a bunch of keys from his pocket and unfastening the padlock. They went inside, but Crannock was out again within a minute. He returned to his van, reversed it over to the storehouse, got out and helped Darmon load several cardboard boxes into the back.

Neal was so intent on watching this operation that he'd failed to spot a third man walking across the courtyard towards the van. Neal's head and shoulders were visible over the top of the wall, and the next he knew the man had yelled a warning to Darmon and was gesticulating feverishly in Neal's direction.

As Darmon looked up and fired off a volley of curses, Neal scrambled down on to the verge and made for his car. He was sure Crannock hadn't seen him, which was just as well. The need to get away was imperative, for he couldn't afford to be recognised.

He heard an engine roar into life on the other side of the wall and knew there was no point in trying to go back the way he'd come. He had no idea where the road before him led and had no option except to continue along it. He moved up through the gears, well ahead of any pursuit. However, he hadn't reckoned on a side entrance to the vineyard. He spotted it at the far end of the wall, as a lorry lurched out into the opening and turned into the road to block his way.

Neal had no choice but to cut his speed. Because of its size, the lorry had had to turn in a wide arc and, as he slowed down, Neal believed he might have a chance to squeeze through the gap between the lorry and the wall. The lorry driver had failed to see that, rolling his vehicle to a halt and climbing down ponderously from the cab. He was a massive, moon-faced bruiser with an ugly scowl. Neal suspected he was as bald as a brick beneath his beret but wasn't going to hang around to find out. As soon as the man was down, Neal trod hard on the accelerator and swerved round the lorry, glad that the skills he'd learned on the force hadn't deserted him. He sped off down the road, a glance in his mirror informing him that the lorry driver was standing in the road shaking a brawny fist at him and doubtless cursing him colourfully.

Before long, Neal came out on to a main road and picked his way back to Valleronde. Making sure to park well away from where Crannock was staying, he stopped off in the square to book his passage back to Southampton on the night ferry and walked back to his *pension*. Tired after the morning's exertions and in some discomfort from his old shoulder injury, he rested, freshened up and headed for the bistro where he'd eaten the previous day. He resolved to stay alert: the last thing he wanted was to run into Bill Crannock.

20

But Neal saw no sign of Crannock that evening. After his meal, he decided to take a last look around the square before returning to the *pension* to pick up his bag and settle his bill. Delacourt's shop had closed some time ago and stood in darkness. He wondered if the antiques dealer was at the Hotel de la Paix, making a nuisance of himself with Sylvie Vernon: he was sure she and her husband would be heading back to Braxbury, if, indeed, they hadn't already gone.

He'd just passed La Paix and was about to leave the square when he sensed a movement behind him. Before he could turn, a heavy hand clamped down on his shoulder, and he was swung violently round to confront his lorry driver friend of that afternoon. The man grinned triumphantly, displaying large, nicotine-stained teeth. He smelt of *pastis* and cigarette smoke.

"So," he growled, "we meet again. Let's take a little walk, *mon ami*."

Neal found himself steered away from the square and its smattering of pedestrians to be led down a deserted side street. The man's hand had landed on his injured shoulder, and he had to grit his teeth to endure the sudden return of pain.

Mistakenly, the lorry driver took his expression for fear and chuckled nastily. For the moment, he was off guard, and Neal took full advantage, balling his fist and turning to sink it into the man's capacious stomach.

The lorry driver made a noise like air escaping from a balloon. His grip relaxed involuntarily, and Neal squirmed away from him, dashing off down the street. The man lumbered after him, his heavy boots seeming to thunder on the pavement.

Neal had kept himself in reasonable shape and felt confident he could outrun his overweight pursuer. Some way down the street, he cut up a narrow alleyway, its mouth partly obscured by tall buildings on either side. His aim was to regain the square, set out in the opposite direction to which he'd been heading when the lorry driver had come upon him, take a wide detour back to his *pension* and make himself scarce. Pausing for a few seconds, he heard no sound of pursuit.

Within minutes, he was back in the square. Evening was setting in, and it wasn't easy to determine people's features at a distance. Then, just ahead of him, a shape materialised out of the gloom which he had no trouble identifying.

They recognised one another simultaneously. The lorry driver cried out, but Neal was already in flight. However, his pursuer was no more than twenty yards behind and, as he caught sight of the church, its imposing spire seeming to pierce the greying sky, he decided he might do worse than try to lose the man there.

He raced through the open doorway. It was dark and cool inside, and on a table below the altar rail, a few candles burned. A slight figure stood beside it and, as Neal came in, began to make his way down the aisle towards him. Neal guessed he was the priest but didn't have the time to introduce himself. The door leading down to the crypt was closed, and he hurried across to tug it open and plunge down the stone steps into a grim and musty darkness.

The moment he reached the floor of the crypt, Neal knew he'd made a mistake. There was no other exit, and the door was taking an age to close, creaking on its ancient hinges. He could only count on his pursuer not noticing it. He crouched behind one of the tombs, knowing his only chance was to remain still and quiet and trust to the darkness to conceal him.

The seconds limped tensely by. The door began to creak again, opening slowly to admit a sliver of grey light. Before ducking back behind cover, Neal caught a glimpse of the lorry driver's face, vast, round and pale, peering cautiously in.

The sight jogged a memory, catapulting him back to that fateful time when he'd glimpsed the killer's face in the warehouse, the dying Clyde at his feet, the split-second before the gun boomed, and its deadly trajectory crashed into his shoulder, flinging him back against the boxes.

Now he felt the old anger and frustration rising in him, the reminder of his weakness, of his failure to identify the man who'd killed his best friend; that friend he'd not only let down but cruelly betrayed.

It was a dangerous anger, almost goading him to arise and confront the man, fight and overpower him, big as he was. A shred of common sense held him back: the man might well be armed – a knife, perhaps – and then what? Images rained in upon him: Wilkie, Roger, Jill. If he was killed or injured in a struggle with the man, how would that help them?

But then the door closed, and he was in darkness again. Why had the man not come down? Was he skulking in the body of the church, knowing Neal was there and waiting for him to come out of hiding? Cautiously, Neal crept out from behind the tomb and stole softly up towards the door.

As he reached the top of the steps, he heard voices raised in argument. Peering through a crack in the door, he saw a small, elderly priest in a dark cassock, probably the figure who'd approached him on his way in. The priest was remonstrating with the lorry driver who, despite being twice his size, stood abjectly before him, kneading his beret in his hands. Neal's French was proficient enough for him to understand that the little priest was admonishing the man for wearing his headgear in the Lord's presence.

In the next breath, the priest pointed a commanding finger towards the main door, and Neal watched as his pursuer trudged disconsolately out, head bowed.

"And don't return unless it's for confession!" the priest railed after him. "It's about time." He watched until, satisfied that the man had gone, he turned and approached the crypt door. Neal stepped back as it swung open. The little priest was smiling. "You may come out now, my son. Your friend won't be back in a hurry."

He studied Neal curiously, as he ushered him out into the church. "You were here yesterday," he observed. "With Pierre Audoin's party. Are you so interested in our crypt, *m'sieu*? Or merely seeking sanctuary from our friend Mallon? Allow me to introduce myself. I'm Father Julien."

"Neal Gallian." They shook hands. "Looking to escape, I'm afraid, Father. There was a near-accident between my car and his lorry. He saw me in town and chased me here."

Julien grinned. "Praise the Lord! Let it never be said that Jules Mallon failed to bring another soul into his church." He shook his head ruefully. "A bad lot, I'm afraid. Would it surprise you to learn that he was once one of my altar boys? I pray for him continually, but so far it doesn't seem to have made much difference."

"I'm grateful for your help, Father," Neal said. "Is there perhaps another way out of here? I have to return to my lodgings before catching the night ferry."

The priest nodded sagely. "That would seem to make sense. Mallon is beyond my jurisdiction out there. Come, I'll show you a back exit. I'm sure you've seen enough of our crypt for one day."

"The guide mentioned the art treasures during the war. The crypt seems to have had its uses?"

Father Julien laughed. "Audoin delights in telling that tale to gullible tourists. I'm sure valuables were hidden away from the Germans during the war. It's well-known that my predecessor, Father Simon, was partial to a good Armagnac and let the Delacourts have the run of the crypt." He broke off, looking aghast at Neal. "Why, my son, what's the matter? Do you feel unwell?"

Neal had put out a hand to support himself on the altar rail. The sudden thought had hit him like a hammer blow, and he had to stop to catch his breath.

"I'm fine, Father," he lied. "It's just that..."

He didn't finish the sentence; couldn't. With the priest's words, he'd been ambushed violently by a suspicion – that was all. Nothing he could prove right at that moment; but, he hoped, he could find proof. Now was not the time. Wilkie, Jill – he had to get back to Braxbury, for their need was urgent.

Julien was looking concerned. He could tell that Neal was troubled.

"Shall I pray with you, M'sieu Gallian?"

"Yes, Father. Yes, please."

They sat together on the front pew, Neal with his head bowed while Father Julien intoned the Hail Mary and Our Father. Once he'd finished, Neal thanked him, rose and lit a candle at the little table. Julien noticed how he stood over it with solemnity and reverence.

Neal remained focused on the flickering flame for a long while, memories and prayers shuttling across his anxious mind.

He had lit the candle for Roger.

21

As the vehicles queued to board the ferry that evening, Neal noticed a gleaming white Citroen DS a few cars in front, and what was unmistakably Sylvie Vernon's elegantly coiffured blonde head in the passenger seat. As luck would have it, he was directed to park two cars behind and elected to stay put until the Vernons had gone up on deck.

But Sylvie spotted him and waved expansively, treating him to another of her dazzling smiles. He had no option but to acknowledge the greeting, making him a sitting duck for Maurice Vernon's scrutiny. The big man, swathed in his favourite overcoat, followed his wife's gaze and scowled at Neal before moving on. Neal hoped the man hadn't recognised him from their brief encounter the previous evening.

He left his car and followed them up the stairs, making sure there were several passengers in front of him. He didn't have a problem with Sylvie – far from it – but didn't want her husband's suspicions of him aroused.

Once they'd reached the passenger deck, Sylvie, with a brief word to Vernon, swept off to the duty-free shops. Maurice met that with a shrug and continued on his way, with Neal staying behind him and well out of his line of vision.

Vernon's destination was the bar. He installed himself at a table and signalled imperiously to a waiter, as Neal slipped behind a pillar. Drinks arrived: a glass of red wine and one of beer. As he sat waiting, Vernon lit up a huge cigar and promptly disappeared behind a cloud of smoke. Not long afterwards, Bill Crannock slouched in, mumbled a greeting and plumped down in the chair opposite the wine merchant.

Neal watched as Vernon drew an envelope from his pocket and handed it across the table. Crannock tore it open, surveyed the contents and made a comment which Neal was too far away to hear. He guessed money had changed hands, and that Crannock had been penalised for the consignment which had gone missing.

Vernon merely shrugged again: he seemed good at that. He growled a response, which didn't cut much ice with Crannock, who picked up his beer, swallowed most of it in one gulp and replaced the glass on the table. He pocketed the envelope and started to walk away, turning at another comment from Vernon.

This time, Neal clearly heard his response. "You needn't worry. I won't make off with it." He stalked out of the bar. Vernon watched him go, then signalled for a second glass of wine. As he turned his attention to the waiter, Neal took the opportunity to slip away. He tailed Crannock but, as he'd expected, the man descended to the lower deck, where he must have reserved a berth for the night crossing. Neal guessed the Vernons would have booked a cabin, so he concentrated on keeping out of their way. He had a meal in the self-service restaurant and installed himself in a secluded corner of the passenger lounge.

He was one of the first to return to the car deck in the morning and settled in his seat, hidden behind a newspaper, snatching a brief glimpse of the Vernons as they returned to their Citroen. Neither seemed in a happy mood. Sylvie was pouting, and Maurice sullen with, Neal guessed, a bit of a hangover. He wondered if they'd had words. He held the newspaper in place until it was time to disembark.

Once off the boat and through customs, he watched the Citroen pull away. It was out of sight by the time they'd cleared Southampton. But he'd decided not to try to keep up with them, as he was sure they'd head back to Braxbury.

It was Crannock who interested him. Neal felt it was highly likely he too was on his way to Braxbury but needed to make certain. He pulled into a lay-by and waited. It wasn't long before Crannock's van trundled past. As it was Sunday morning, there wasn't much traffic on the road, so Neal kept a good distance behind, not wanting to be recognised.

Once in Braxbury, he parked at the top of the main street and walked down the hill. Watching from across the street, he saw the van drawn up outside the storage shed behind Vernon's shop. A door slammed, and Maurice Vernon emerged from the house, approaching Crannock, who was leaning idly against the wall.

Vernon rapped out an instruction, and Crannock left his post and slid open the van's side door, his movements slow and contradictory. Vernon wasn't pleased, and as the house door slammed shut again and Sylvie appeared in the courtyard, he took out his frustration on her, ordering her back inside. She went, but not before offering Crannock a twinkling wave and seeing his glum features finally yield to a smile. There'd been something deliberate about her gesture.

Vernon waited until Sylvie had gone before unlocking the storage shed door. He and Crannock unloaded the van in silence, carrying a succession of boxes into the shed. Neal didn't think there'd be much else to see and, anxious to avoid the soon-to-depart Crannock, headed back to his car.

He drove down through Braxbury and out to Briar Hedge, uncertain as to what greeting he might get from Jill Westmacott but needing as well as wanting to see her again.

She'd heard his car turn in, for she was at the door as he pulled up, wearing a blue and white summer frock and a welcoming smile which held a hint of apology.

"Oh, Neal. Thanks for calling round. I've been trying to ring you. Please, come in."

She stood aside to let him pass. He hovered hesitantly in the doorway, not sure if he was completely forgiven, for they'd not parted on the best of terms. Jill, for her part, seemed equally uncertain. They ended up briefly hugging, and both stumbled inside.

Jill invited him to take a seat, which he did, then stood in front of him, smiling ruefully.

"I didn't know if you'd want to see me again?" she said shyly.

"I wasn't sure you'd want to see me," he replied cautiously.

He noticed that her eyes were moist behind her lenses, but she was smiling. "And I'm sure that I do," she said.

He scrambled to his feet and took her in his arms; held her close, and it felt so good to hold her, absolving himself, absolving them both.

"Oh, Neal, I was so horrible to you. I – I was afraid you'd gone off somewhere to get away from me. I rang your number every day. I think your landlady got fed up with me."

"She's fed up with everyone," he said. "You mustn't take it personally."

"She said you'd gone to France and had no idea when you'd be back."

He imagined Mrs Pendle's morbid glee as she'd uttered those words. 'Negative' was her middle name.

"I went to Valleronde," Neal said. "I needed to ask some questions about Roger."

"Valleronde?" Jill drew back, surprised. "But didn't Sylvie Vernon –?"

"I know. I ran into her over there. She told me about the body in the summerhouse. It was such a relief to learn that it wasn't your uncle's."

"A tremendous relief." She looked up at him wretchedly. "But it makes me feel even worse about the way I behaved towards you. I – why I think I may have *scratched* you -?"

"Shall we say you left your mark?"

She hung her head. "I'm so sorry. I can't believe I was so childish."

He put his hand beneath her chin and tilted her face up towards his. "You were probably in shock," he said gently. "That's understandable."

"Even so -?"

"Even so, nothing." He pulled her close again and kissed her. He thought at first that she was somewhat taken aback, but then she responded to him, pressed her body into his.

When, finally, they drew apart, she smiled up at him. "I think you must have forgiven me."

He returned the smile. "There was nothing to forgive."

Jill led him by the hand into the kitchen, offered him tea and they sat together, drinking companionably. He thought it was about time they got talking about other matters.

Neal was going to have to broach the subject of Colonel Wilkie's whereabouts but didn't think it was quite the moment. He asked instead if Tomkins had succeeded in identifying the body?

"Yes," Jill replied eagerly. "And Tomkins seemed to think I should know him, simply because he was found in our summerhouse. Yet the name meant nothing to me."

"Then who was he?"

"They're treating it as murder – he'd been stabbed. They only managed to identify him from some items in his wallet." Jill looked at him, puzzled. "It wasn't a name I recognised. Apparently, the man was called Manning. John Manning."

22

Neal was glad he was sitting down. For several moments, he was numb with shock, incapable of speech. The suddenness of the name, the way Jill had uttered it, for it was unfamiliar to her, all contributed to his mute astonishment.

Jill had drawn back from him in alarm. "Oh, Neal, I'm so sorry. You must have known him…"

Eventually, he gathered his wits. Speech returned to him, his words sounding dazed and hollow. "Yes. Yes, I did."

For it had happened how he'd suspected, how he'd feared. Manning's departure from the Ormsbys' caravan had been an abduction. And it had led to murder.

Jill was looking at him anxiously, an uncertain hand on his. He clasped it firmly, with relief. He had to confide in her. Jacko's death begged the question: *where was Lambert Wilkie?* There was all the more reason he couldn't mention that now, for he had a more pressing matter to consider. He'd confided in Wilkie, and in doing so might have placed him in danger. Perhaps he was about to consign Jill to the same plight, but he doubted she'd thank him for keeping her in the dark any longer.

"There are things you need to know," he said decisively. "I've told your uncle, and it's only right that you should be aware of them too."

Neal told her how he'd known Jacko Manning from his time in the police. He hadn't seen him since he'd put him inside and had been surprised to find him in the Farmers the other evening. That had been just over a week previously: it seemed longer.

Jacko had explained that he'd happened upon an old army pal from the war, Ted Stoker. After a spell together in North Africa, they'd gone to different postings, and Stoker had been in Colonel Wilkie's company in Normandy in 1944. He'd been one of the reconnaissance party, which had gone up to the Chateau Garay after the Germans had fled and had witnessed Roger Gallian's disappearance. But, well into his cups that evening at the Chasing Hound, Stoker had declared that there'd been something wrong about Roger's desertion, implying that he might not actually have deserted at all.

"Naturally, I was keen to have a word with him, but when Jacko and I met him at the Hound the next evening, Stoker clammed up and dashed off. Jacko was nearly run over twice by someone driving a van, a Commer or something similar, which was when you showed up and rescued me. The following day, I took him to hole up with some friends of mine in a village near Cirencester. I didn't think we'd been followed, but someone got to him and whisked him off. Now he's turned up dead." He looked at her earnestly, taking her hand in both of his. "I'm loath to drag you into this, Jill. But it strikes me you're in it anyway, and…"

She interrupted, raising her free hand to silence him. "Please, don't apologise, Neal. I needed to know, and Uncle Lam's told me nothing of this." Her pale features lapsed into a sad smile. "Like you, I dare say he wanted to protect me. But the time for that's past. As things stand, I'm in a quandary. Did someone want us to think the body in the summerhouse was Uncle Lam's, or was it actually a warning to him?"

Neal couldn't answer that. Indeed, he felt uncomfortable. After all, where *was* Wilkie? He attempted to mask his unease by turning it into a question. "I suppose you've heard nothing from him?"

It was Jill's turn to look uncomfortable. "Sergeant Tomkins is keen to talk to him," she replied anxiously. "He believes Uncle Lam may know something about the – the body. But really, I -," she looked at him appealingly, "I don't see how he can?"

She was looking bewildered and, having overcome his initial awkwardness, he took her in his arms again, and they hugged fiercely.

"Thank you, Neal," she whispered.

"What for?"

"For taking me into your confidence."

"You've a right to know. It concerns your uncle."

"Well, that and – well, thank you for just being here. I don't know if my tantrum the other day deserves it."

"That's in the past," he replied. "And forgotten by me. You must forget it too."

They kissed again, their mutual shyness and reserve also forgotten. When they finally had to come up for air, Jill was once more wearing her serious expression.

"You said you'd been to Valleronde, Neal. Did you find out anything there – concerning your brother?"

He shook his head. "Not really. I sought out the resistance man who'd gone up to the chateau with the recce party, but he couldn't add anything to what I already knew."

But it hadn't been altogether a lost cause. Vernon, Crannock, the pick-up at the vineyard. The reaction he'd got there, and later from the lorry driver, Mallon, in Valleronde: all that involved something more than a few missing bottles of wine. Neal felt bad about it but really couldn't let Jill in on any of that, at least not for the time being. There was, after all, no proof of any wrongdoing, and he didn't want to risk her saying anything to Sylvie, with whom she was friendly.

Jill forestalled him anyway. She got to her feet, looking decisive. "Neal, there's something I must tell you. But first, well, would you like a spot of lunch? There are a couple of pork chops in the fridge, and I can boil up some potatoes."

He realised he'd not eaten since the previous evening on the ferry. "That'd be great," he grinned. "But only if you let me help."

They spent a happy time together working in the kitchen, but as they sat over their meal, he could tell there was something more on Jill's mind. He asked if she felt she could share it with him.

She smiled at him warmly. "You're right, Neal. I need to share this with someone, and I'd rather it wasn't Sergeant Tomkins. But you see – I've heard from Uncle Lam."

"You *have*?" He was shocked all over again, although not into speechlessness. "But that's tremendous news! Where is he?"

"He phoned early this morning, asked if you were back yet. That was why I tried phoning you, because he's got important information, and he's asked for you to get in touch as soon as possible."

"What sort of information?"

"He wouldn't say. But he wants you to meet up with him."

"He's not coming back here, is he? It probably wouldn't be a good idea."

Jill shook her head. "No, of course not. He wants you to go there."

"Where?"

"Auntie Marj – his late wife – owned a cottage in Lincolnshire. When she died, years ago now, because I never knew her, it passed to him, and he's never been able to bear to part with it. It's a bit out of the way, although he uses it from time to time and occasionally rents it out to old army friends and the like. All he said was that he intended to hole up there for a while, and that I should keep telling Tomkins I'd heard nothing from him. Uncle Lam wants you to go there as soon as you can."

"That'll be this afternoon, then," Neal decided. He wondered if the information Wilkie had might have something to do with Manning's death. He believed it all linked up with Roger anyway. "Where do I find him?"

Jill set down her knife and fork and drew a slip of paper from a pocket in her frock, handed it across the table to him.

"I've drawn you a map. It's rather remote. Three or four miles off the A15 north of Bourne. It's called Marlam Cottage. They lived there when they first married."

She was looking perplexed as she watched him stow the map away in his blazer pocket, and he asked her what was wrong.

"Well, it may be nothing. But I had to draw that map from memory. Uncle always kept the directions over in that sideboard. An Ordnance Survey map marked with the location of the cottage – Mum and Dad have used it when they've gone up that way. But when I looked, I couldn't find it."

"Perhaps it's just been mislaid."

"Possibly. Uncle Lam's not the tidiest person, but when I looked for the map, the drawers were in a terrible muddle. I'd tidied them up only last week. And he kept a gun in there, hidden at the back of a drawer. It's not there now – although I suppose he might have taken it with him."

He asked the question which had immediately sprung to mind on her mentioning the missing map. As for the gun, it was highly likely Wilkie had taken it.

"Do you think someone else might have been through those drawers? Maybe while you were staying up at Sylvie's?"

"I don't know. It would have been easy enough for someone to break in. A couple of window catches at the back of the house are loose – I just hadn't got around to tightening them. Then again, the map might have been in his desk in the summerhouse and got destroyed in the fire."

"But you don't think so?"

"And neither do you."

He grinned tightly. "You're right. I don't. And if I'm going up to Lincolnshire, I'd better get started. Jill, as a precaution, you ought to make sure the doors and windows are properly fastened."

"Thanks, I will. But -?"

"What?"

"Neal, can't I come with you?"

She was looking at him pleadingly, and he considered her request for a full two seconds.

"It's best if I go alone, Jill."

Her shoulders slumped, her disappointment plain as she toyed absently with the food left on her plate. He decided that he had to trust her, as she'd trusted him. With Wilkie out of the picture – he hoped temporarily – she was his only ally. He leaned towards her.

"Jill, listen. I need you to go back to work at the shop."

She looked up sharply, her interest fired by the note of urgency in his tone.

"When I was in Valleronde," he went on, "I ran across Maurice Vernon. He met up with Bill Crannock."

She frowned. "That's nothing unusual. Mr Vernon buys direct from several vineyards in the region, and Bill goes across to fetch it for him. There are a number of customers over here who purchase heavily, including my uncle."

Neal told her about the previous morning, when he'd followed Crannock to the *Vignoble Darmon*, and how he'd not been welcome.

"I believe I've run across a smuggling operation," he concluded.

Jill looked crestfallen. "Oh, but surely Bill can't be involved?" she cried. "He can't let Uncle Lam down – he helped Bill set up the carrier business when he lost his way a few years ago."

Neal was interested now. "What? Through drink?"

Jill nodded solemnly. "That and gambling, I think. Uncle really believes he's turned the corner, and Bill has always seemed so grateful to him."

"How do you get on with Maurice Vernon?" Neal asked.

She looked doubtful. "I can't say I like him. Sylvie and I run the shop between us, and thankfully he's often away on business."

"My impression was that he's not a particularly pleasant man."

Neal guessed she had more to say. She looked away, then turned back to face him, gnawing at her lower lip. He waited patiently for her to speak.

"He – made a nuisance of himself once," she explained, her voice a whisper. "He'd been drinking – it was one of the few occasions when he and I were alone in the shop. Luckily, Sylvie came back early and sent him packing."

"I'm sorry." Neal reached across and took her hand. She smiled back at him sadly.

"I felt such a fool," she said. "I think – well, I don't know what Sylvie thought."

"Did she say anything to you afterwards?"

"No. She never mentioned it. Almost as if it had never happened. Obviously, they don't get on. It would never surprise me if they divorced before long."

"Let's go back to Vernon and Crannock in Valleronde. This meeting they had wasn't at all convivial. Remember that man – our friend in the green hat – who came into the shop last week?"

"Yes. D'you know, I believe I've seen him around with Bill."

"Well, he's lit off with some consignment. I'm sure it's what we witnessed the other night, and I doubt that it's wine. Vernon was incandescent and blamed Crannock because he'd brought the man in. It's my guess the missing consignment contained drugs, and that Vernon suspects Crannock and Green Hat might be in this together."

"So, what do you want me to do?" Jill had recovered from her embarrassment and seemed keen to help.

"I need you to be my eyes and ears in the shop. See if you can pick up anything which might give us a clue as to what's in those boxes. But for heaven's sake, Jill, don't take any risks."

23

She accompanied him out to the car, and by that time he was wishing he'd allowed her to come to Lincolnshire with him but believed it was more important that she stayed to keep an eye on what Vernon and Crannock were up to.

Her hand had slipped effortlessly into his and, as he swung open the driver's door, he turned, swept her into his arms and kissed her. There was nothing tentative on either side now, and he drew her into a firm embrace.

They were both so preoccupied that they could only have half-heard the soft crunch of a footfall on the gravel; but the unmistakable sound of a clearing throat was enough to make them spring guiltily apart.

Sergeant Tomkins stood a few yards away, a lewd grin on his face. "Sorry if I'm interrupting," he said.

Neal heard no hint of apology in his remark, and Jill looked furious rather than uncomfortable. He squeezed her hand, and she gave back the pressure. He guessed a show of temper would have made Tomkins' day, if, indeed, they hadn't just made it already. Previously, the jury had been out, but at that moment Neal realised that he really didn't like the police sergeant.

"Where've you been off to these last few days, then, Mr Gallian?" Tomkins tried to inject a matey tone into his question, but his mean little eyes gleamed nastily from beneath the peak of his cap.

"Across to Valleronde," was Neal's terse reply. Tomkins looked bemused, so he added, "It's in France. I met up with someone who was with my brother before he disappeared."

"Oh, right." Tomkins had to prevent himself dismissing the response with a shrug. He wasn't at all bothered with that. "So, you've not by any chance been in touch with Colonel Wilkie?" He'd tried but summarily failed to sound off-hand.

"Hardly. I've only just learned from Jill that it wasn't his body in the summerhouse. And that, in fact, it was Jacko Manning's."

"Hhmm, yes. Puzzling. But no great loss in my opinion. Did you ever -er, make his acquaintance?"

"I nicked him once, a few years back. Ran into him again not all that long ago. I can't say I disliked him. So, what's your theory?"

Tomkins puffed out his chest. Neal had been certain he'd have a theory because his sort always did: the frustrated ace investigator.

"In my opinion, one of his dodgy mates did him in – and he'd have had plenty of those. We've spoken to his employer and his landlady. They seemed to think he was on the straight and narrow. But take it from me, his sort doesn't change, even if he'd managed to steer clear of trouble since coming out of clink." Looking officious, he turned to Jill, seeming to tower over her. "Now, Miss Westmacott, have you received any communication from your uncle since we last spoke?"

This time, Jill squeezed Neal's hand, and the gesture reassured him that she wasn't at all fazed by Tomkins' overbearing attitude. Indeed, she lied superbly. "No, Sergeant. He's not been in touch at all, I'm afraid."

"Well, if he does, you must be sure to let me know right away."

"I will, I promise." Butter wouldn't have melted, and Neal had to fight hard to suppress a grin.

"Same goes for you, Mr Gallian." Tomkins' warning bore a hint of menace, making Neal wonder if he suspected they were keeping something from him. "As you well know, it's a criminal offence to withhold information from the police."

Neal nodded soberly, and Tomkins, flashing him a suspicious look, touched the peak of his cap to Jill, turned and crunched back out to the lane, where he'd left his car.

Once he'd gone, and the sound of the Hillman had faded away, Neal took his leave of Jill, each of them a little more restrained in their goodbyes after having been embarrassed by the sergeant. It was a long drive up to Lincolnshire, but Neal made good time to Bourne; although once he'd passed through the town, things became a little more difficult.

To say that Marlam Cottage was off the beaten track was an understatement, as Neal managed to drive past the opening to the lane, down which he eventually found it, no less than three times. In general, however, Jill's instructions had served him well.

He turned off down an un-signposted narrow track through a tunnel of leafy trees, which practically obscured it from the road. He could make out a tiny cottage something like a quarter of a mile down. The lane wound on past the cottage heading nowhere in particular, and Neal drew his car up on to the grass verge, just beyond a bend.

Marlam Cottage was in need of some maintenance: its thatch was grey and worn, door and window frames thirsty for paint. As he pushed his way through the front gate, which had collapsed on its hinges, Neal glimpsed something hidden behind the bushes to the side of the property, a dull green which didn't quite match the shades of the undergrowth.

He made his way over and discovered, deep in the shrubbery, an ageing Land Rover. He'd made a mental note of the registration number the other day at Briar Hedge and knew it was Wilkie's. The engine was cold, the door unlocked, and a quick search inside revealed nothing. Neal returned to the cottage.

Its front door was unlocked too. Stepping into the little hallway, he called the colonel's name, but nothing came back. He started to look around. The furniture showed signs of age, and he guessed Wilkie and his wife must have lived there before the war. The table, sideboard and dresser all bore the same shade of scratched, tired oak. In the sitting room, one armchair and a sofa were shrouded with dust sheets, but a second armchair, next to the ash-strewn fireplace, was uncovered.

Neal went upstairs. There was nothing in the wardrobe, but the sheets on the bed were thrown back, as if it had been recently used, and on a shelf in the bathroom sat soap, a razor, brush and shaving cream.

There were further signs of habitation in the kitchen: a dinner plate, knife, fork and mug in the sink, tins which had contained Irish stew and baked beans in the bin and a half-empty carton of milk on the table. Neal sniffed at the milk: it had gone off in the warmth of the afternoon.

All this begged the questions: where was Wilkie now, and was he coming back? Outside, the light was fading, and it was gloomy in the cottage. Neal wondered if he should wait. Suddenly, he tensed, as he heard a sound beyond the front door. He'd closed the rickety gate behind him and had heard it being pushed open, its bottom scraping slightly on the path. He ducked into the hallway, keeping back from the windows. A heavy footstep thudded on the path. Could it be Wilkie?

Or someone else?

A second later, he realised that, once again, he'd been outdone by indecision. Whoever was on the path had hesitated, probably having spotted his car pulled up on the verge beyond the bend. Too late, Neal lunged for the door and yanked it open. The visitor had gone, the shiver of branches indicating that he'd plunged into the undergrowth rather than escape up the lane.

Neal gave chase. He was in reasonable shape, but the fugitive had a head start and wasn't hanging around. Some distance ahead, Neal made out a mad crashing through the shrubbery. He glimpsed the road beyond the screen of trees and bushes. The light was worsening by the minute, although for a moment he could pick out a running figure silhouetted against the glow of the setting sun.

But several seconds later, the only noise he could hear was of his own making. He didn't slacken pace, increasing it instead, as there was a chance the fugitive might have tripped over a root and gone sprawling.

And that was his undoing. He glimpsed the shadow-shape close by a split-second before a heavy branch was catapulted into his face. He was knocked off balance and went down in a heap, must have blacked out for seconds, his face stinging, for the fugitive was careering off through the shrubbery again.

Neal struggled to his feet and blundered along in pursuit, reaching the road sooner than he'd expected. He peered down it, as he heard a door slam. There, some fifty yards away, he made out the squat shape of a van, as the engine kicked into life, and it accelerated off into the gloom.

Giving chase was useless. Neal returned to the cottage, brushed off the dust and leaves and splashed cold water on his face. Then he went back to the car and started the long return journey to Oxford.

He had a lot on his mind. Nothing was clear, and the incident at Marlam Cottage had muddied the waters still further. The questions remained: where was Lambert Wilkie?

And what was the important information he had for Neal?

24

It was late by the time he got back to his flat. The day had been busy with a lot of driving, and he'd not had much sleep on the boat the previous night, so it was mid-morning by the time he'd washed and breakfasted. If he'd not been fully awake, Mrs Pendle's impatient tattoo on his door would have completed the job.

"Phone, Mr Gallian!" she shrieked. "Your woman again."

He thanked her on his way down, presuming she hadn't been referring to Flo Ormsby. But it was, as he'd hoped, Jill. She sounded harassed.

"Oh, Neal, thank goodness. I was afraid you might not be back yet."

"I didn't get back till late, Jill. You okay?"

"I'm phoning from the shop. Sylvie suggested I call you. Can you come out?" She lowered her voice, although he suspected Sylvie Vernon kept a more respectful distance from other people's telephone conversations than his esteemed landlady, who was pretending to dust the banisters less than three yards away. "There's something I need to ask your advice on."

"That's fine. I can be with you in about three-quarters of an hour."

"Oh, thanks, Neal. I'll see you then."

*

It was past midday by the time he'd parked in the High Street and walked down to the shop. Sylvie must have been on the lookout for him, for she had the door open to admit him. She looked stunning in a tight black skirt, high heels and a lacy blouse, which wasn't quite opaque.

"Neal, how lovely to see you." Her eyes twinkled mischievously, as she latched on to his arm and escorted him into the shop. "My dear, we have a very glum young lady here, who's clearly worried about something. So, I suggested she phone you."

Jill was tidying shelves near the counter at the back of the shop. Beyond her, a side door led out to a small customer car park, the shed where the boxes from Crannock's recent visit to France had been stored and the Vernons' house and lawn behind the leylandii hedge.

She looked up and smiled nervously, and Neal found himself reluctantly comparing the two women. Sylvie was glamorous: not quite beautiful, but she'd long ago discovered the art of knowing how to make the best of herself and was supremely confident in her dealings with men.

Jill, in her calf-length, floral-patterned skirt and sandals, looked, if anything, a lot younger than her years. Studious in her glasses and ponytail, she nonetheless possessed a freshness, which the other woman lacked and could no longer attain, and was undeniably pretty. He had the impression, too, that Jill wasn't as recalcitrant as she might at first appear to be. He guessed that if Maurice Vernon had persisted in his crude advances, he might have been in for a shock.

"I think Neal should take you out to lunch and cheer you up," Sylvie declared.

Jill reddened slightly but hung on to her smile. "Thanks, Sylvie."

"Mind you, you must promise to be back on the dot of two o'clock," she added. "I need to be in Oxford by three."

"But I'm never late, am I?" Neal caught the welcome hint of challenge in the girl's reply.

"Of course not, dear." Sylvie spoke placatingly, and then the twinkle returned. "But you may get distracted in the company of this handsome man. I know I should be." She laughed as Jill's blush deepened. "Well, at least that's lent her a little colour. Off you go, both of you. Enjoy a nice, leisurely lunch." She turned to Neal. "I can recommend the Queen's Head at the top of the High Street."

"Thanks," Neal replied. "We may well take you up on that."

Sylvie smiled at him winningly, caressed his arm again and hugged Jill, as she collected her handbag from behind the counter.

"Have fun!" she trilled, as they left the shop.

"I'm sorry about that," Jill murmured, once they were out in the street. "Sylvie can be very sweet, but at times extremely embarrassing."

"I think she means well," Neal replied lightly and, once they were out of Sylvie's line of vision, took Jill by the hand.

He'd deliberately drawn the line under that last subject, because privately he couldn't be sure where Sylvie Vernon had been coming from. He'd got the impression that she'd been trying almost to belittle the girl. For his own part, he admired Sylvie, who was undoubtedly a good-looking woman. But he felt she sought to establish a controlling influence over Jill, possibly because too often, in her own case, she had to let her husband call the shots.

"I -er, hoped you might have called in on your way back last night," Jill said cautiously, as they walked up the hill.

"It was very late," he said lamely. He wondered if, in her shy way, Jill was offering him an invitation to go further. After all, it was what he wanted. He'd been hampered by Helen's ghost, by his own shame and ineptitude for far too long; above all, he needed someone who believed in him, capable of lifting him from his past-ridden torpor.

Jill nodded distractedly, and he felt sure she hadn't misinterpreted his words as a rebuff.

"Neal, I really need to talk to you. Do you mind awfully if we don't go for a meal? Can we just buy a sandwich from the bakery over there and go up to the park? It's on the left at the top of the hill. You'll have seen it on your way in."

"That's fine by me."

He bought sandwiches and a pastry each, and they walked up to the park. It was a fine day with a light breeze, and they found a vacant bench in the shade of a clutch of rowan trees, bright with their bouquets of orange berries.

As they settled themselves, Jill started speaking. Even though there wasn't a soul nearby, her voice was close to a whisper, and Neal had to lean across to hear her.

"Did you get to meet up with Uncle Lam last night?" she asked.

"No," Neal replied. "He wasn't at Marlam Cottage. But he'd been there – I found his Land Rover hidden in the shrubbery. My guess is that someone came looking for him, and he got out quickly some time before I arrived. Probably the same person who showed up when I was there."

He told her about the visitor to the cottage, how he'd given chase and lost him.

Jill looked alarmed. "My goodness! Who do you think it might have been?"

"I don't know. He made off in a van."

"Not – not a Commer van?"

"The light was fading, and it was some distance away. I couldn't swear to it. Why? Do you think my visitor might have been Bill Crannock?" Neal was intrigued. He hadn't thought of Crannock: the idea gave way to new possibilities.

And Jill's next words introduced another. She was looking troubled.

"I wasn't thinking of Bill. Mr Vernon's got a van too – it may not be the same make, but the colour's similar to Bill's. He uses it for deliveries."

"Then it could be either of them." Neal was puzzled. He couldn't think what connection they'd have with Wilkie to the extent of – presumably – wanting him out of the way. He didn't particularly wish to broach the subject, because he felt he might end up upsetting Jill, and she was vulnerable enough at present anyway.

But Jill saved him the bother by changing tack. "Neal, there's something else." She sighed. "Sergeant Tomkins has been to see me again this morning. Almost made me miss the bus to work, and they only come along at two-hourly intervals."

That seemed typical of Tomkins, in Neal's opinion. "What did he want?" he asked.

"He seemed suspicious. Asked me if I had any idea at all where Uncle Lam might be. And did I know if he'd known the man who was killed – Manning? He was trying to find out if there was a connection. Neal, I couldn't answer this, but do you happen to know if Manning served in France with my uncle during the war?"

"The colonel told me he didn't know Manning – and he had a good memory for the names of the men in his company."

"Then why do you think he's run away?"

She seemed agitated, and Neal felt he had to let her down lightly.

"Possibly because someone's looking for him, and it wouldn't be a good idea for him to be found."

"But who could it be?"

"That's what we must find out, Jill. And we have to find your uncle before the police do."

She caught the implication behind his words and looked at him sharply. "What do you mean by that?"

He took a deep breath. "Because a man's body was found at his house after a fire, and he's disappeared. Jill, when your uncle phoned you, can you be absolutely certain it was *his* voice you heard?"

She bridled at that. "Neal, what on *earth* are you saying?"

He held her gaze, working hard to withhold a smile, because he was glad to witness the spark in her. He'd been right: she was no shrinking violet.

Jill realised that he was trying to help and immediately climbed down. "I'm sorry, I'm feeling a bit tense."

"I understand."

She frowned thoughtfully. "You're right. I suppose I automatically assumed that it was his voice. Come to think of it, it sounded a bit muffled, although the line wasn't good." She glanced at her watch. "Goodness, it's already ten to two. We'd better get back, or Sylvie'll be in a flap."

"We'll talk some more later. If he phones again, tell him to get directly in touch with me."

She agreed to do that, and they walked back through the park. But Neal was worried. He tried not to show it, but he felt weighed down by an avalanche of questions. *Could Wilkie somehow be involved?* Someone had silenced Jacko Manning. Could it be because he'd started the ball rolling, and someone had felt it necessary to put him and Stoker out of the way?

And apart from the smuggling issue, how might Crannock or Maurice Vernon be involved?

25

"Neal, is there something you're not telling me?"

Jill's voice broke in upon his preoccupation and pulled him up sharply. She sounded a little suspicious of him, and her expression was anxious. He immediately felt guilty, reminding himself that he'd decided to confide in her. He didn't think she'd be too impressed if he tried to explain that he'd been awaiting the right moment with the intention of letting her down gently.

"Sorry, Jill. I'll be open with you. I still believe that all this has something to do with my brother's disappearance. I believe your uncle's played straight with me, but the very fact that he's disappeared suggests he's involved too. Jacko Manning and Stoker – where it all began – are both dead. So, what is it that Colonel Wilkie knows? And why has he disappeared?"

"When you say he's involved, what exactly do you mean?" Jill's voice had suddenly taken on a hard edge. He supposed that there'd been an implication in his words that Wilkie might not be on the side of the angels. It had to be a possibility, and one which she needed to bear in mind, because things wouldn't be so difficult for her if it turned out to be true.

But she was stung, and once more he was encouraged by her fighting spirit, even though she wasn't exactly looking on him favourably at that moment.

"And what about Roger?" Neal had been trying to form a diplomatic answer to her question, but she didn't give him the chance to speak. "Mightn't he be *involved*? Mightn't he even be at the back of what's going on? Have you given any thought to that?"

"I don't believe Roger was a coward or a deserter," he replied. But he knew the words lacked passion. Because Jill had effectively stopped him in his tracks, made him wonder for the first time: had he been wrong to believe so implicitly in his brother's innocence?

But no, no, he was sure he'd been *right*. His thoughts went back to the crypt in the church at Valleronde, to the sudden possibility which had overwhelmed him then, choked him: that Roger was in no position to answer for himself.

Jill strode ahead of him, purposefully making for the shop's side door. He guessed she was angry and, if the situation hadn't been so serious, might have been amused by her indignation.

Neal quickened his pace to get in front, so that he could open the door for her. She
flounced into the shop ahead of him without a word of thanks, then pulled up abruptly with a gasp, causing him to clatter into the back of her.

Raised voices were coming from the office at the back of the shop; Sylvie Vernon's voice shrill, tinged with panic, the man's gruff and implacable.

"Maurice, don't be so hasty. He's worked for you for years, always been so reliable. Can't you -?"

"He's worked for me for the last time. I'm determined to have it out with him. He's been *cheating* me, him and Slant. Are you so dense you can't get your head round that? And how long's it been going on, that's what I'd like to know? And it's what I'm going to find out and put a stop to."

"Well, in any case, you won't need that. For God's sake, put it back in the drawer."

"I need it to make him see sense. You took that phone call. You know what they're like."

"Maurice, I had no idea what you were into..."

"*No idea?* Where the hell do you think all the money comes from? This is a serious matter, you stupid woman. A matter of life and death – for *me*. And now, if you don't get out of my way, I swear I'll knock you down!"

They stumbled out into the shop. Sylvie tried to block his path, her hands on the door frame, but Vernon was in no mood for delay and barged into her, sending her skittering back against the counter.

Only then did they notice Neal and Jill looking on anxiously from the doorway. Sylvie looked shocked and embarrassed, but there was no reaction from her husband, mean and taciturn as he brandished a gun carelessly in his right hand.

Neal stepped forward calmly, placed his hands upon Jill's shoulders and moved her gently aside, making sure that he stood between her and the gun. "The police take a dim view of men who push their wives around, Mr Vernon," he remarked.

Vernon glared at him. "Who the hell asked you?" he growled. "Get out of my way."

"Neal." Sylvie looked scared. "*Please* – you'd better do as he says."

Her husband cast her a savage glance over his shoulder. "On first name terms, eh? Who's he – another of your *admirers*? Bloody town's infested with 'em. And don't think I don't know about your little dalliance with Crannock. That's something else I owe him for." He appraised Neal bleakly. "Oh, yes. You were in Valleronde, weren't you? Trailing around after us. Well, my friend, I don't know who you are or what your business is, but -," he waved the gun under Neal's chin, "you and your little girl had better move away from that door. If you go on blocking my path, you'll get something you didn't bargain on."

Jill gasped again, and her hand clamped on to Neal's arm, trying to pull him back. He didn't need persuading. They shuffled backwards, away from the door. Vernon levelled the gun at his chest, as he moved towards it.

"And stay where you are, all of you," he snarled. "This is between me and Crannock."

With his free hand, he pulled a key from his jacket pocket, backed out on to the driveway and locked the door. Neal watched as he made his way round towards the garage. He'd had the vague idea, as he and Jill had come in through the side door, that there'd been two vehicles outside, but he'd been preoccupied by Jill's animosity, and his view had been anyway obscured by the bushes.

A door slammed, an engine kicked into life, and Vernon drove past the shop door. He was driving a dark blue Morris van, near enough in size and colour to be reckoned, in the dark and at a distance, to be Bill Crannock's green Commer.

Jill had released her grip on his arm, and suddenly Sylvie was clutching the other. She looked frazzled and seemed to be blinking back tears.

"Neal, he's in such a dangerous mood. We *have* to stop him. *Please* – follow me." She headed purposefully for the street door, and Neal, gently detaching his arm from Jill's numbing grasp and trying to reassure her with a smile, went after her.

"Jill!" Sylvie rapped, as she tugged open the door. "Call the police – now! If it has to be that man Tomkins, then so be it. Send them to Bill's warehouse down by the old mill. And for God's sake, make them hurry! Maurice is going to – oh, I can't believe he means it!"

They dashed out on to the street and round to the driveway.

"What's all this about, Sylvie?" Neal demanded, as they made for Vernon's Citroen, which had stood alongside the van.

"I'll tell you on the way," she snapped. "Right now, we've got to – oh, *hell*!"

On the point of opening the driver's door, she pointed down at the Citroen's front tyre. It was flat. "Damn him! *He* did this – he knew I'd go after him."

"My car's up the street," Neal offered. "And you were about to explain?"

They hurried back to where he'd parked his car. "Drugs trafficking," Sylvie gasped breathlessly, stumbling in her high heels, as he took her by the arm and hustled her along. "It's been going on for years, apparently, and he's kept it hidden from me all this time. I had my suspicions on the last couple of trips, then this morning I took a phone call. Maurice ripped the receiver from my hand, but I'd already got the gist of what the caller was saying.

"Bill Crannock and a friend of his, Phil Slant: they were the delivery men. Bill brought the consignments across, and Slant took them on to their destination. Maurice had suspected for a while that between them they were creaming a little off and selling it on, but now a whole consignment's gone missing. Some man's been phoning every day for a week, it seems, and this morning I've never seen Maurice in such a rage. He was scared, too, because the man must have threatened him. That's why he's decided to have it out with Bill once and for all."

By the time Sylvie was through, they were at the bottom of the hill and turning into a narrow lane which opened to reveal several barn-like warehouses. Outside one of these stood Vernon's and Crannock's vans. The Morris had almost ended up in the side of Crannock's Commer, and Vernon had left the driver's door hanging open in his haste to confront Crannock.

Neal drew up behind them and was quickly round to the passenger side to prevent Sylvie impetuously rushing in.

Holding her tightly by the arm, he led her to the open door of the warehouse. Crates and boxes were stacked to one side, and beyond them a metal staircase led up to a small office on a gantry.

On the floor below it, Maurice Vernon's body lay face down and splayed out, blood pooling beneath him, his gun in his outstretched hand.

While Bill Crannock knelt beside him, dumbfounded, as he stared up at them unseeingly. And Neal and Sylvie stared in horror at the second gun, which he clutched in his hand.

26

Sylvie screamed, snatching her gaze away from her husband's body and covering her face with her hands. She swayed slightly, and Neal flung a supportive arm around her shoulders, afraid she might faint.

"Oh, Bill," she sobbed. "Why – *why* did you do this?"

Crannock looked up at them, but Neal wondered if he saw them. He seemed to be in shock, his mouth working at words without the voice to utter them. Neal thought about disarming him but had his hands full with the distraught Sylvie, and Crannock didn't seem to pose a threat. The gun dangled loosely in his grasp, and he stared at it in stupefaction, as if he couldn't think how it came to be there.

Neal had no idea how long they remained frozen in that grisly tableau. As the strident sound of a police car's siren woke him from his stupor, he wondered if it might have been scarcely any time at all. But they seemed to have arrived promptly, and he was glad of that.

Footsteps sounded in the doorway, and he looked round to discover a wiry, dark-haired man in a gaberdine mac, accompanied by a sullen-looking Sergeant Tomkins.

The first man had a lean face and quick, intelligent eyes beneath thick dark brows. He busily took in the scene before him, the brows knitting together in something like astonishment, as his gaze finally came to rest on Neal.

"PC Gallian," he exclaimed. "What the blazes are you doing here?"

In more fortunate circumstances, Neal might have grinned on observing the flash of resentment on Tomkins' face, as it registered the fact that Neal knew one of Oxford CID's 'confounded whizz-kids'. But most of all, he felt relieved. Detective Chief Inspector Don Pilling could hardly be described as a 'kid', but Neal had worked under him before and knew him to be fair-minded.

"It's a long story, sir," he replied.

"I'll bet it is," Pilling remarked drily. "Miss Westmacott's been in touch," he went on. "But I dare say you know about that. Told us to get along here quick. Too late, clearly."

Sylvie, clinging to Neal, finally raised her anguished face. "I told her to phone," she said. "The dead man is my husband, Maurice Vernon. He came down here to see Mr Crannock. He was angry with him – had a gun. I don't know what he intended to do, but I was scared there'd be bloodshed. I asked Mr Gallian to come with me, hoping we might be able to prevent any trouble, but..." She glanced down tearfully at Vernon's body and the immobile Crannock. "Sadly, we arrived and found – oh, dear God!" She turned her face away and buried it in Neal's shoulder.

Gradually, Bill Crannock had become aware of voices and people around him, hemming him in as he crouched over Vernon's corpse. He looked bemused, still holding the gun by its handle.

"Take it off him, Sergeant," Pilling ordered, and Tomkins edged uncertainly round to the far side of Crannock, reached out and grabbed at the gun. There was no resistance, and Tomkins pulled it effortlessly from his grasp.

"Carefully does it," Pilling groaned. "We'll need to check it for prints." He drew a large envelope from his pocket and handed it across to Tomkins. "Okay," he told Crannock. "On your feet."

The big man hauled himself up and stood with his head bowed. Neal ushered Sylvie away, so that the two policemen could get either side of him. He heard a car screech to a halt outside, followed by running footsteps, then two fresh-faced, uniformed officers appeared in the doorway.

"Ah, nicely on cue," Pilling greeted them.

"We were in the area when we got the call, sir," the first man said.

Neal didn't recognise them and suspected they were based in Witney unless they'd started at Oxford after his enforced departure. They both looked like they'd not long left school, and he was beginning to feel as though he was getting left behind.

At last, Bill Crannock found his voice. He looked up imploringly, first at Sylvie, then Pilling. "I was in the office up on the gantry," he said. "Vernon came rushing in through the open doorway, waving his gun and bellowing my name. Then suddenly this other geezer appeared behind him – I mean, he was just *there*. Vernon half-turned, and this bloke shot him, threw down the gun and scarpered." Pilling was looking unmoved, and Crannock's protest moved up a few notches. "Listen, guv'nor, that's how it happened. I *swear* it, and I swear it wasn't me who topped him. *Please* – you've got to believe me!"

Pilling grimaced. "We'll have to see about that, Mr -?" He glanced inquiringly at Tomkins.

"Bill Crannock, sir. He's the local carrier. Sir, this isn't like him at all. I've known him for some time."

Pilling sighed, unimpressed. "Just do the honours, Sergeant. Character references can come later."

Tomkins nodded uncomfortably, conjured handcuffs from somewhere about his uniform, reached over and clamped them on Crannock's uncomplaining wrists.

Crannock looked hurt. "Oh, come off it, Tommo. You *know* me. Listen, mate, you know I'd never do anything like this…"

Tomkins stared back stone-faced, intoning the caution in a sepulchral voice.

"Take him out to the car, Sergeant," Pilling said. He watched the two men leave before turning to one of the young constables. "Right, lad. Get on your radio and get the pathologist and scene-of-crime boys over from Oxford, then hang about here till I get back. You know the form." He glanced at Sylvie, who'd fastened on to Neal's not altogether unwilling shoulder, her face drawn, and eyes averted from her husband's body. He addressed the other constable. "And you can run Mrs Vernon home." He looked at Neal. "I take it she lives nearby?"

"The Leylands in Braxbury High Street," Neal replied. "Miss Westmacott's waiting there. She'll look after her."

"Okay." Pilling turned back to the constable. "You wait there too, until I get one of my people out from Oxford to take a statement from Mrs Vernon."

The young constable approached uncertainly, and Sylvie looked up at Neal, aghast. "Wh-what's happening?"

"The constable's taking you home, Sylvie. Don't worry, Jill's there. She'll look after you." He addressed the young man. "You'll need to explain to Miss Westmacott what's happened."

"I'll make sure to do that, sir. This way, madam."

Sylvie threw them both a wan smile and allowed herself to be led away.

Pilling had been watching this exchange with something like wry amusement.

"That leaves you and me, Gallian. Got your car here?" Neal affirmed it with a nod. "Good. You can follow us back up to Braxbury. Tomkins and I'll get Mr. Crannock sorted, then you and I can have a chat."

"Right, Mr Pilling."

The DCI grinned tightly. "And you can explain to me just how you happen to have turned up at this particular crime scene. Can't keep away from the job, eh?"

Neal wasn't so sure about that, although Pilling had been one of those, along with his old sergeant, Tom Wrightson, who'd tried to persuade him to return, once he'd recovered. But the wounds had been too many and had gone too deep. He guessed the DCI, in his late forties now, would have seen it all before and understood.

He followed Tomkins' Hillman into Braxbury, where it pulled up outside the police station, a grim, red-bricked Victorian villa at the top of the High Street. Neal parked behind them, was shown by Pilling to a seat in the drab reception area and watched as he and Tomkins escorted Crannock into an equally unprepossessing room opposite. That left him with the grey-haired, unsmiling constable who was manning the inquiry desk. A long wait revealed that he was non-speaking too.

Finally, Neal heard sounds of movement from the interview room. The door opened, and Tomkins hove into view to ask his colleague to accompany 'the prisoner' to a cell. Once he'd disappeared with a still bemused Crannock down the passageway to the rear of the building, the sergeant glared at Neal. "You're to come through," he muttered wearily, not bothering to disguise his animosity.

Neal got up and squeezed past him into the room, where Pilling was waiting. "Organise some tea for us, Sergeant," he drawled, as he pointed Neal to a chair. "Then that'll be all for the time being."

"Yes, sir."

Tomkins withdrew glumly. As Neal might have wagered, when the tea arrived it was brought by the unsmiling constable and tasted like it had been strained through an old sock. But by then Neal wasn't too bothered about the tea.

"Okay, Gallian." The DCI's manner was business-like. "What's your take on all this, and how do you come to be involved? We've charged Crannock with Maurice Vernon's murder. I'm having him transferred to Oxford nick shortly. So come on, lad. Let's hear what you have to say."

Neal was confident that he could speak freely in front of Pilling, one of the few senior officers who'd sought and valued the opinions of the uniforms who'd arrived first on the scene of his investigations.

"The way I see it, sir, is that someone's setting this up. I believe Crannock's innocent of Vernon's murder. I take it he's coughed up to the drug-smuggling operation? Mrs Vernon told me about it on our way down to the warehouse. Her husband only owned up to her this morning, after she'd taken a phone call intended for him."

"Oh, Crannock's admitted to that," Pilling said. "And there's more to come on that score. But it goes a lot deeper than a piddling little drugs scam, doesn't it, Gallian? Your involvement in it, I mean?"

"You're right, sir." Neal had long ago decided not to hedge; he wanted Pilling on his side. "I'm pretty sure it's got something to do with Roger."

"Your brother?" The DCI had shown an interest three or four years back. They'd been on a stake-out and had got talking.

"Yes." He took a deep breath and gave Pilling the whole story from that night, more than ten days ago now, when Jacko Manning had shown up in the Farmers looking for him.

"I think I know where my brother is, sir," he concluded. "And Bill Crannock knows it too. It's a place he's never left."

The DCI took it all on board. Neal couldn't tell whether he was with him or not, but you never could with Pilling. However, he promised he'd have a thorough session with Crannock once he'd got him to Oxford.

He went on to explain that he'd been at Briar Hedge that afternoon with Tomkins. Jill had given them her permission and in fact had phoned them there, which explained their prompt arrival at the warehouse.

"Would you say Colonel Wilkie was on good terms with Crannock?" Pilling asked.

"The colonel's his ex-CO from the war. He helped Crannock out when he got into financial difficulties a few years back. I'd say there's a mutual loyalty if not friendship there. Jill – Miss Westmacott – can probably give you more details."

Pilling leaned on the table and fixed Neal with a penetrating stare. "Gallian, do you think there's any likelihood of Wilkie and Crannock being involved in this together? Wilkie's disappeared, and no-one seems to know where he's gone. Might he possibly have gone on the run?"

Neal could imagine the fireworks if and when Pilling put the same question to Jill. He'd put it to her himself in a roundabout way because the same possibility was very much on his mind. He dreaded finding the answer. But for now, under pressure from Pilling, he answered as best he could.

"I don't know, sir. I like Colonel Wilkie and really hope he's not involved."

The DCI studied him darkly from beneath his thick brows. "You were in the job long enough to know that 'like' doesn't come into it, Gallian," he remarked grimly.

Neal returned to Oxford, having promised to contact Pilling if he had any further thoughts, or if anything else came up. It was well after eleven o'clock as he climbed the stairs and let himself into his flat.

He sensed immediately that something was wrong: a slight movement in front of him in the darkness. He dashed on the light and tensed.

Colonel Lambert Wilkie sat in an armchair facing the door. There was a gun in his hand.

It was levelled unerringly at Neal's chest.

27

"Come in," Wilkie said. "And close the door."

Neal did so and stepped to one side. The gun tracked his movement.

"I was wondering when you might show up," he remarked. "By the way, how did you get in? I take it Mother Pendle didn't invite you in for supper?"

"If by that you mean the angular, rather sour-faced woman who went off up the street at about seven-thirty, then no, I waited until she was long gone."

"She doesn't go out much. You were lucky it was her bingo night."

"Just as well, then." Wilkie lowered the gun. "There was a sash window open at the back. I made the devil of a row shinning up the drainpipe – out of practice by some forty-odd years. Fortunately, the room I entered turned out to be yours."

"If it had been Mrs Pendle's, you'd have just escaped a cool reception."

Wilkie allowed himself a tight grin. "Hardly bears thinking about." He was quickly business-like again, relaxed his grip on the gun. "How's Jill?"

"Extremely confused. And she's not alone."

"Sit down, Gallian."

Neal sat at the table, facing him. Wilkie looked unkempt, his hair greasy and tousled, chin bristling with several days' beard. His clothes were rumpled, looked slept-in, which was probably the case.

"You look tired," Neal said.

"I am. Desperately." Again, the grin, as Wilkie carefully set down the gun on the arm of his chair and leaned back in it. He nodded towards the table, and Neal's gaze lit upon a plate containing a few crumbs. "Hungry too. My apologies, Gallian. I'm afraid I helped myself."

"No objection. So, Colonel, why did you leave Briar Hedge in such a hurry?"

"Staying there would have been bad for my health. Late on Tuesday afternoon, when Jill was at work, I took a phone call. I didn't recognise the voice – a man's – offering me information concerning your brother. I was to go to some remote location – a disused mill on the Windrush several miles away. I was immediately suspicious; more so, when I discovered I had to park at the roadside and take a footpath across fields which passed through a small copse. I guessed my anonymous caller would be concealed in there, and he was. He took a pot-shot at me, which must have missed by a mile, and I got out quickly before he could take better aim.

"I didn't return home. If someone was out to get me – although heaven knows for what reason – I wasn't going to give him another chance. I'd held on to a cottage in Lincolnshire, which had belonged to my late wife and decided to hole up there until I could make contact with you. I phoned Jill, but she was unable to reach you."

"I was over in France – Valleronde," Neal explained. "Seeking information about Roger."

Wilkie nodded. "I thought I'd be safe up there – Jill was the only one who knew about it. But somehow, he or they managed to catch up with me – I can't think how."

"I can," Neal said. "When I called on Jill, she asked me to go up there. She was going to show me the location on a map kept in your sideboard. It had gone, and I suspect someone had broken in and found it before Jill got back from work. It looked as if someone had been riffling through the drawers."

Wilkie looked grim. "That would explain everything. Well, I hiked into the village for a few provisions, and when I got back to the cottage the night before last, someone was waiting. Whoever it was didn't see me, and I made off on foot with only the clothes on my back and this old service revolver, which had belonged to Marjorie's father. Discretion rather than valour: I couldn't tell if our friend was alone."

"He came back when I called in there," Neal said. "I surprised him, and he made off in a hurry." He didn't mention the van, as he couldn't now be sure whether it had been Crannock's or Vernon's.

"I got back to Briar Hedge by various means," Wilkie went on, "and found the summerhouse burnt to the ground and police everywhere. What exactly is going on, Gallian? It's beyond me."

Neal told him: about Jacko Manning's body, his visit to Valleronde and its consequences, the drug-smuggling operation, Vernon's murder and Crannock's arrest.

He could see that the colonel was struggling to take it all in. "But is Jill safe?" he asked earnestly.

"I left her in Braxbury this evening. She's keeping Sylvie Vernon company."

Wilkie sighed. "That poor woman. It's well-known that she and Vernon had a rocky relationship, but it must have been a hell of a shock for her to lose him like that. Gallian, do *you* believe Bill Crannock killed him? Seems out of character to me, and I've known the man for twenty-odd years."

"No, sir, I don't. I think he's been set up, and that he's telling the truth about the man at the warehouse. *He's* Vernon's killer – and it wouldn't surprise me if he's tied in with the drug-running business."

"Any ideas who he might be?"

"I'm afraid not. But the police aren't thinking along those lines." Neal paused weightily. "They're looking for you."

"Ah." The colonel showed no surprise. "Something to do with my friendship with Bill, I don't doubt. That, and the fact that I was never too keen on Maurice Vernon. The man was a charlatan in my opinion, and Jill has told me how obnoxious he was towards his wife. I suppose it's a logical path for them to take. Have they been here?"

"Not yet, to my knowledge. But I've been closeted with the senior officer this afternoon, DCI Pilling. I can tell you from experience that he's no slouch."

"Then I dare say he'll be here before long." Wilkie flashed Neal a quick glance. "I believe we're up against someone very clever, my boy. Someone wants me out of the way, and if I'm implicated in these dealings with Bill or with Vernon's murder, that's as good as immobilising me altogether. I think our friend's been tracking my movements. When he took that pot-shot at me, he never intended to hit, just scare me into going on the run, which would be an admission of my guilt, to all intents and purposes. Now, here's the big question: *why?* I believe I have an idea of the answer."

Both men started at a frenzied hammering at the house's front door.

"That'll be Pilling," Neal said.

Wilkie got to his feet and handed him the gun. "A pity. I'd hoped to have longer with you. They'll be here, no doubt, because of one of those 'anonymous tip-offs'. He'll have guessed this is somewhere I might go. Gallian, listen, because time's short. I've had some time to think, and I believe I know why the summerhouse was razed to the ground. You must hand me over now, for your own sake, but I beg you: take care of Jill." His words came rapidly, urgently. "Ask her to look out the address for my old colleague Johnnie Vosper. It should be in a drawer in the sideboard. He lives in North Yorkshire and he's not in the telephone directory. Poor old boy's in bad shape, but he has the memory of an elephant. Ask him the name of any soldier who may have gone missing when his platoon was ambushed at Pont du Garde, where my man Harry Doyle – remember him? – was killed. I can't explain now."

Mrs Pendle's bedroom door slammed shut, and they heard her hurrying downstairs, muttering peevishly about what time of night did they think it was?

They heard her unlock the front door, ask the same question aloud and find that the callers weren't about to go meekly away.

Footsteps thundered on the stairs and, with a wry smile, Wilkie took a step towards Neal. "We'd better make this look good."

Without hesitation, Neal got up and clouted him on the jaw. Wilkie gasped, tottered back and landed violently in the armchair, whose springs twanged furiously. The colonel managed another brief grin, as he nursed his aching jaw. Neal whisked up the gun, turned and snatched open the door.

DCI Pilling and two large uniforms spilled in.

"I should imagine you're looking for Colonel Wilkie, sir," Neal greeted him respectfully. "He came calling here. In fact, he burst in and threatened me." He held out Wilkie's gun by the barrel. "You'd better take care of this."

Pilling eyed Neal curiously and, with a half-smile, took hold of and bagged the gun.

The colonel groaned from the depths of his armchair. "Blast you, Gallian. You've got this all wrong. Why won't you listen to me?"

The DCI walked up to Wilkie and stood over him. "I'll listen to you, Colonel, and I'm sure there are a few issues you can help us clear up. Issues such as Bill Crannock, an aborted drug-smuggling operation, and the sudden death of Mr Maurice Vernon, where it appears that the gun used turns out to be yours. It may take some time. Perhaps you'd come along with us."

Wilkie scrambled to his feet. He bore the appearance of a degenerate old tramp but managed to look suitably indignant. "I have no idea what you're talking about, officer," he protested, as the uniforms hustled him away.

"Good work, Gallian," Pilling complimented him. "Apologies for adding to your overlong day, but I shall need you to make a statement."

"I'll come right along," Neal said. He followed them downstairs, smiling reassuringly at the petrified figure of Mrs Pendle, who remained at the front door, still holding it open and gaping in astonishment.

28

It was well into the early hours when Neal arrived home from the police station, letting himself in quietly to avoid waking his landlady. He'd made statements regarding his involvement in the incident at Crannock's warehouse, as well as the arrest of Lambert Wilkie. DCI Pilling informed him that he'd sent one of his officers along to the Leylands the previous evening to obtain a statement from Sylvie Vernon.

After a few hours' sleep, Neal went down to the hallway, taking advantage of Mrs Pendle's morning foray to the corner shop to use the phone. He called Briar Hedge but got no answer, so presumed that Jill had stayed with Sylvie overnight.

He phoned there, and Sylvie picked up almost immediately. It was hardly surprising that she sounded subdued. Yes, Jill was with her: she'd stayed overnight at Sylvie's request and had been a great comfort. The police had called again that morning – that awful Sergeant Tomkins.

Neal wondered if he could come over and see Jill: he needed to talk to her.

"I'm sure she'd be delighted to see you, Neal. Please, come over as soon as you like."

He said he'd start right away. Despite having lost her husband not twenty-four hours previously, Sylvie's words had nonetheless held their habitual teasing nuance.

She answered the door to him, glamorous in mourning, a simple black suit, white blouse, court shoes and exquisite make-up, which was in no way overdone. She hugged him closely, her body pressing against his for an intimate moment. He guessed the delicate perfume she wore might have come from the expensive *parfumerie* in the square in Valleronde.

Neal offered his condolences on the loss of her husband, and Sylvie looked suitably solemn.

"Poor Maurice," she said wistfully. "Our marriage wasn't happy, but we were full of hope once and, I suppose, in love. It didn't last." She sighed. "I shall sell the business, of course, and probably return to France. It was always Maurice's, rather than mine. I doubt if I shall re-open the shop at all."

She led him through to a wide, airy lounge, complete with stereo system and television in light oak casing and long, low-slung, Swedish-style sofas. Jill was sitting primly on one of these, ponytailed and demure in her summer frock, cardigan and spectacles; the perennial girl-next-door. But as soon as Neal appeared, she sprang to her feet and hurried across the thick-pile white carpet to greet him.

They came together in a slightly hesitant embrace, due entirely, he felt, to Sylvie's presence. She invited them to sit, offered coffee in a belated attempt to leave them alone for a few moments; but Neal refused it, instead inviting Sylvie to stay. She sat on the opposite sofa, looking a little apprehensive.

Neal seated himself beside Jill. He felt her hand trembling in his. She'd sensed that his visit was hardly a social one.

"I'm afraid the news is disappointing," he said, hoping somehow to cushion the blow. "Jill, your uncle's alive and well. However, he's been arrested and is currently being held in custody in Oxford."

"Then why did that stupid Tomkins not bother to tell us?" Sylvie thundered.

"He probably didn't know," Neal replied. "He was back in Braxbury – Colonel Wilkie was arrested in Oxford."

"My goodness." Sylvie shook her head disbelievingly, got up and moved across to crouch in front of the girl, taking her free hand in both hers.

Jill hardly seemed to notice, staring dumbfoundedly at Neal. "*Arrested* Uncle Lam?" Her voice was scarcely above a whisper. "But, Neal, whatever for? What's he supposed to have done?"

Neal hesitated for a moment, before realising that there was no easy way to put it.

"They suspect him of aiding and abetting Bill Crannock, both in the drug-smuggling operation and the murder of Maurice Vernon."

Sylvie looked up, her eyes flashing. "*Colonel Wilkie?* But that's ridiculous. How could he be involved? Huh! These policemen – what do they have between their ears? Sawdust?"

Jill shook her head in confusion. "Neal, it's just so crazy. I can't believe it."

"You say he was arrested in Oxford," Sylvie went on. "Did he go to them and give himself up?"

Neal paused, looking thoughtfully at them both. He couldn't throw off the impression that Sylvie was overreacting and wondered why that should be? He guessed his next words would light the fuse as far as Jill was concerned.

"No," he said. "When I got back late last night, Colonel Wilkie had broken into my flat. The police arrived and arrested him there."

This time it was Sylvie who was taken aback, and Jill who reacted. A spot of colour had appeared high on each cheek, as she'd taken the information on board. For a moment, she seemed unable to move or speak, her lips pressed tightly together, eyes staring fixedly at the far wall. But only for a moment.

Then she angrily flung off Neal's consoling hand, turned in her seat and faced him squarely.

"Do you mean to say," she demanded in a dangerously low voice, "that you actually stood by and *let* them take him away?"

Her naivety betrayed her youth. Neal held up a calming hand. "Jill – I didn't exactly have a choice."

Sylvie's face appeared as she leaned across the girl. "I'm sorry, Neal, I thought you knew the main detective who came to the warehouse. What was his name? Pilton?"

"You *do*?" Jill's voice was shrill with accusation. "Neal, I just can't believe this! If you know the man, why the – why the *hell* couldn't you have put in a word?"

"I think it would be asking a lot, dear." Neal had wondered how long it might take for Sylvie to see reason. "We *are* talking about the police here. They can be a bit inflexible."

"And it's not as simple as that," Neal added. "The reason I'm here is to take you to see him."

"Well, I should hope so too!" Jill stood up abruptly, stalked over to the window and looked out at nothing, simply so that she could turn her back on him. "After what you've done – or haven't done, well, it's the very least I'd expect!"

At that moment, the telephone in the hallway rang, and Sylvie hastily excused herself to go and answer it. Neal was glad of the interruption. He wanted to talk Jill round and could attempt it a lot better without Sylvie in the room.

"Your uncle's going to need a few things," he said. "Perhaps we could call in at Briar Hedge on our way. And Jill – please – trust me. I think there may be a way out of this."

Taking courage in both hands, he stood and went over to join her at the window, placed a tentative arm round her shoulders. "Yes," she replied distractedly. "I'd better put a bag together for him – pyjamas, toiletries, that sort of thing."

She appeared to have calmed down, but Neal sensed she was still simmering inside. He was glad she hadn't pushed him away again, although there was still time. He tried to withhold a grin, failed and was rather glad she couldn't see it.

Because he liked the fire in her. She wasn't so naïve that she'd let anyone pull the wool over her eyes. She might be very young but was certainly her own woman and would need that strength and more in the days ahead.

Sylvie had been talking volubly on the phone. The conversation had been in French, in low, urgent tones; and as he and Jill had stood at the window, Neal had caught the odd phrase: "Later today, then. Yes, come here."

Sylvie now reappeared in the room, looking a little flushed. She smiled the moment she saw their gazes upon her.

"My apologies for that. My mother. She didn't know, of course. I've just explained to her. She had a soft spot for Maurice."

Neal didn't buy that. Her mother – coming *here*? Doubt must have shown on his face because Sylvie was looking at him somewhat suspiciously.

Jill spoke, claiming her attention. "Sylvie, Neal's driving me to Oxford. I need to see my uncle."

Sylvie had lost some of her previous spontaneity. "Of course, my dear. You must go. I can't help thinking this is all one big mistake."

"I think so too," Neal replied.

He was rewarded with a sharp glance from Sylvie, tried to hold her gaze, but she looked quickly away, all her attention for the girl.

"Go with Neal, my dear." She enveloped Jill in a hug and thanked her for her support.

"I'm sorry to leave you like this," was Jill's parting comment, as they all walked towards the door.

"There's no need to worry about me," Sylvie reassured her. "I'll be all right."

Neal was glad he was looking elsewhere as Sylvie spoke. Because of that, he was sure.

29

He'd left his car on the street and, as he and Jill walked down the driveway, he sensed Sylvie watching from the lounge window.

Jill did too, for she turned and waved, smiling. The smile had faded by the time she'd turned back to walk alongside him, and he realised that she was still angry with him. They reached the car, got in, and he drove down the High Street and out of Braxbury.

Jill sat sullenly beside him, staring dead ahead. He switched her a glance. "Let's talk this out, Jill," he said quietly. "What am I supposed to have done wrong?"

She still wouldn't look at him. "You know full well what it is," she replied tetchily. "I simply can't believe you just let them arrest him without at least speaking up for him. I thought..." There was a catch in her voice.

"What did you think?" he asked gently.

She looked towards him at last, his quick, sideways glance registering the gleam of tears behind her spectacles. She suddenly seemed very young and extremely vulnerable.

"Well, that – well, you and I..." She didn't finish the sentence and, her face aflame, looked away. When she resumed, she was studying the floor and had taken a different tack. "Look, he *can't* be guilty of what they say, simply *can't*; not Uncle Lam. Neal, he likes and trusts you and – and you've let him – let us both down. Can't you understand that?"

"Jill." His voice was quiet but firm. "Your uncle *told* me to hand him over."

He *what?*" He had all her attention now, as she stared at him, wide-eyed in disbelief.

"He didn't want me implicated. There was no point in us both ending up in a police cell. And yes, I know as well as you that he's not guilty. He's been set up. I believe it's because someone suspects he may be on to something; and you and I have to find out what that is and who they are."

By this time, they'd reached Briar Hedge. Jill let them into the cottage, and he followed her into the sitting room, where he told her of Wilkie's suggestion that they contact Johnnie Vosper.

"I've heard Uncle mention him," Jill said. "His address should be in one of those drawers. He lives somewhere up in Yorkshire – Northallerton, I think. Ah, here it is." She handed Neal a small address book. "Uncle Lam told me he'd been crippled in the war and can't get down to their reunions very often." She threw up her hands in despair. "Oh, I can't get over how muddled everything is in these drawers."

"That's because, as we'd previously suspected, someone's been riffling through them."

"What?" She looked up, alarmed. "The police have been here: I gave them permission to look around. Then – do you mean someone else?"

Neal nodded. "Definitely someone else, and before the police got here. I'd guess the intruder was after the address of Marlam Cottage; also, that he or she had found it. Which would explain why Colonel Wilkie had to leave there in a hurry. You also mentioned a gun at the back of one of those drawers."

"Yes, that had gone, and we wondered if Uncle Lam had taken it."

"I don't think he did." Neal kept his voice steady, laid a supporting hand on her arm. "The person who's trying to frame him took it. You see, Jill, it was used to kill Maurice Vernon."

"Oh, my goodness." She'd turned pale, and he led her over to the sofa and sat down beside her.

"And that was partly why the police have arrested him," Neal explained.

"Then we've got to prove he's innocent," she said decisively, snapping out of her trance. "Is that why he wants us to get in touch with Colonel Vosper?"

"We're to ask him a question." Neal told her what it was, and she looked puzzled; as puzzled as he felt, but he wasn't questioning Wilkie's motives. "And I'd like you to go to Yorkshire and call on Vosper, Jill. First off, though, I'll take you along to Oxford nick to see your uncle."

Jill faced him squarely, looking rueful. "Neal, I have to apologise once again – for flying off the handle; for not trusting you, when I can see now that I should have trusted you all along."

He smiled reassuringly. "That's all right, Jill. I'm sorry I was so mysterious about it. But it was for a purpose."

He thought she might ask him what that purpose was. She didn't, and he was glad of that, because, coming on top of her uncle's arrest, it might have been too much for her to bear. And in any case, she was in his arms by then. How he wished that she could have stayed there, because then he might have a chance of keeping her safe, as Wilkie had asked him.

However, time was pressing. Neal helped her pack a few items in a small suitcase for her uncle and got her to sort out an overnight bag for herself. As they set off, he advised her that, when she got to see Wilkie, there'd be someone monitoring the interview, so to keep the conversation on an elementary level and show concern for his well-being. He left the content to her but made her understand that she should convey a message from him that everything was in hand.

Neal waited outside in the car, while Jill went in to see Wilkie. She emerged reassured that he was all right and more than ever convinced of his innocence. The colonel's instruction to her had been to trust Neal implicitly.

"You realise we're being watched, don't you?" he said, as they drove away.

"What? By the police?"

He shook his head. "Someone else."

She looked worried. "But I've not noticed anyone."

Neal grinned. "I can't say I have either. But it's a safe bet that we are, and we need to give them the slip."

"How do we do that?"

"I'm going to draw them off, while you take a train to London, then up to Yorkshire. I want you to see Vosper and ask the question. Then," he handed her a slip of paper, "phone this number and ask for DCI Pilling. Give him my name. Here's some money for the train fare, and now, Jill, just act naturally and follow my lead. We'll call in at my flat first."

They found a parking space halfway down the street and walked back to the flat hand in hand. At the sight of Jill, Mrs Pendle's face assumed its classic disapproving look, and her manner was frosty to the point of rudeness. Neal explained that the young lady was a family friend who was stopping off briefly before resuming a long journey, and he was going to offer her a cup of tea and a sandwich. His approach was polite but firm, and Mrs Pendle gave way.

"You'll be so good as to leave your door open, then, Mr Gallian," she observed tartly, in a stage whisper which Jill, halfway up the stairs, had no trouble overhearing. "You know my Rules."

Neal made tea and put together a snack, all the while conscious of his landlady restlessly prowling in the hallway. Jill seemed amused by the situation, and he was glad of the distraction, for he knew matters were coming to a head, and it was imperative that she caught the next express train for Paddington.

They left the flat under Mrs Pendle's relentless gaze and walked up the street and round the corner to the Farmers. It was early evening of a dull September day, and he was glad that darkness would fall swiftly. He kept his arm around Jill's waist as they walked, alert to the sound of any pursuit; but all he heard was the light slap of their own footsteps on the wet pavement.

In the predominantly male preserve of the Farmers tap room, Jill's trim figure collected numerous admiring glances. Neal installed her in an unpopulated corner with a Pepsi, and a double scotch for himself, before asking Herb if he could use the phone behind the bar.

He called a local taxi driver he'd known for a few years, who agreed to bring his car round to the pub's back yard in ten minutes.

They'd finished their drinks and were outside waiting when the taxi drew up. Their parting was briefer than he felt either of them might have wished, and he could tell that Jill was apprehensive of undertaking the long journey alone.

"Good luck," they said simultaneously, smiled nervously at one another, and then she practically threw herself at him, kissed him on the lips and clung to him briefly. Moments later, she was in the back seat of the taxi, waving goodbye as it drew away.

Neal went back inside. "Young lady friend, Mr Gallian?" Herb enquired casually, as he polished glasses behind the bar.

"The niece of an old acquaintance," he replied readily, as Herb pulled him a pint of mild and bitter.

"And very nice too."

Herb had never been one to be too inquisitive, but Neal felt bound to offer a fictitious explanation for the cloak-and-dagger incident the landlord had lately witnessed.

"Sorry about all that," he apologised. "She was worried that an ex-boyfriend, who'd been making a nuisance of himself, had followed her to Oxford this afternoon."

"Ah, I see," Herb replied ruminatively. "Well, I can't say I'd blame him for that."

30

Neal stayed in the Farmers for a chat with Herb and a couple of regulars, had another half of mild and bitter; deliberately spinning things out, killing time.

It was after eight-thirty when he left, by which time Jill should be well on the way to Paddington. A steady rain was falling, but he doubted it would have proved too damp for whoever was waiting for him outside.

For of that, he was sure: someone was.

Neal turned the corner into his street. It was very quiet. Cars were parked all down one side, their roofs and bonnets twinkling with beads of rain in the muted glow of the streetlamps. As he drew nearer to Mrs Pendle's front door, he heard the click of a car door opening. A few cars down, a figure emerged slowly from the driver's seat, a tall, deadly silhouette in the gloom.

The figure moved unhurriedly around the car and walked up the narrow pavement, blocking his progress. She'd thrown a black leather coat over her white blouse and black suit of the morning. It was worn carelessly, like her smile. She watched him appraisingly as he moved towards her; cautiously too, because she couldn't be sure how he'd react.

"Good evening, Neal." Her tone was light-hearted, seemed to hold an invitation.

His reply was studied and level. She couldn't have known how long he'd been on his guard, anticipating a meeting.

"I won't ask what you're doing here, Sylvie. But I did wonder when I might run into you again."

"Oh? You did?" Her response was pert, flirtatious. It was dangerous too, especially as her smile remained. "Well, Neal, I'd like you to come with me now."

"And if I refuse?"

"Then I'd have to insist." She pouted briefly. "But I'm sure you wouldn't make me do that?"

Neal wondered then if she might have a gun, but he saw no handbag over her shoulder, and her arms hung loosely at her sides. He decided she was armed with nothing but her sexuality, which was powerful enough.

She reached out and latched on to his arm a little uncertainly. When he didn't resist, she started to lead him down the street, past the tenuous lifeline of Mrs Pendle's door.

"My car's just down here." She looked up at him curiously. "But you don't seem at all surprised by my waylaying you so suddenly?" She sounded disappointed.

"I'm not. There've been certain things which have made me wonder about you for a while."

"Oh, that's a pity. There was I thinking I'd been so careful. What might they have been, Neal?"

"The evening of the fire at the summerhouse. How did you know there was a body? Only Jill and I had been round to the back of the cottage. And the day your husband was shot - you were a mite too insistent that Jill should be back at the shop on the dot of two – a girl who was always punctual. It marked the start of the performance: you were quarrelling with Maurice as we walked in. Then there was the slashed car tyre. He wouldn't have had time to do that. You'd already done it, giving your accomplice plenty of time to get to the warehouse, shoot Maurice and disappear before we arrived there. Which nicely set up Bill Crannock for his murder."

"An accomplice?" Sylvie sighed. "Oh, Neal, you make me sound like the original scarlet woman."

"I'd describe you more as dangerous than otherwise, Sylvie," he replied.

She drew them to a halt beside the Citroen. It had probably been Vernon's car, but it was hers now. Neal wondered briefly if part of the motive for Maurice's death had been that all he'd owned would pass to her. The sale of the business alone would fetch quite a sum. She was a designing woman and clever with it. He had the idea that she'd planned all this. But why? He guessed he would soon find out. And after that, he would know too much. Then he'd have to take his chance.

He was playing a dangerous game: the risks were high. But he felt strangely comforted. Cautious by nature, there'd been times, in his police days, when he'd taken risks, had had to; followed by that one occasion when he hadn't, that occasion he'd regret forever. It felt almost good to be risking his life again, and he took heart from it. For Jill's sake, for Wilkie's, it was the right thing to do.

Sylvie was feigning innocence. Her grip on his arm felt cloying. All the time he believed she was playing cat-and-mouse with him; and there were no prizes for guessing whose role was which.

"But surely, Neal," she protested, "the police have arrested Colonel Wilkie for my poor husband's murder?"

"And you know as well as I that he didn't do it."

"And yet was not Maurice killed by a bullet from the colonel's gun?"

"He was, Sylvie. But then, how would you know that, because it's not general knowledge?"

She nodded graciously. "Oh, my, I am so careless." She gripped his arm tighter, and her expression grew serious. Perhaps he glimpsed a hint of genuine regret unless it was just one more illusion in a night of shifting shadows.

"It's a pity, Neal. That's all I can say. A great pity." She pressed up close to him, as she'd done once before, and kissed him gently on the cheek. But her exquisite perfume smelt sickly now, and he was totally impervious to her charms, knowing that it had been a traitor's kiss.

"However, you're right. Colonel Wilkie didn't kill Maurice. That was someone else."

He must have been concealed in one of the doorways, masked by the darkness. For as Sylvie stepped away, Neal was aware of a soft movement behind him, followed by the uncompromising prod of a gun between his shoulder blades, and a voice he recognised but could scarcely believe he was hearing.

"Evening, Mr G. What brings you here, then?"

And Neal turned to stare into the insolent, grinning face of Jacko Manning.

31

"Better come along with us nice and quiet," Manning quipped.
"Hey, didn't you say that to me once upon a time?"

"What the hell's going on, Jacko?" Neal growled. He was confused; wasn't sure whom he'd expected to see. Certainly not Manning, but here he was, as large as life, and his involvement sparked off a whole cavalcade of questions in Neal's mind.

"Reckon you said that too. Once a copper, eh? Must be a heck of a hard habit to break."

Sylvie had finally relinquished her custodial grip on his arm: that, at least, was some consolation.

"And now tell us what you've done with dear little Jill, Neal?" she asked teasingly. "Didn't you want to keep her with you? I thought the two of you were so close?"

"She had to leave in a hurry," he replied tersely. "An urgent family matter."

"Ah, I see." Sylvie and Manning exchanged a brief smile, which Neal saw and distrusted.

Manning prodded him with the gun again, as Sylvie swung open the Citroen's rear door. He got in, Manning behind him, while Sylvie slid in behind the wheel and drove off. Very little was said. Neal was aware of a gloating grin on Jacko's impudent face. He'd dearly have liked to wipe it off, but there was the gun to consider. He sat quietly, awaiting an opportunity.

It came as they drove out of Oxford. Sylvie seemed unfamiliar with the city – London was probably more in her line – and instead of heading out north via the Woodstock Road, she'd gone west through Botley. Neal presumed they were returning to Braxbury; in which case, they'd need to cut across country to get to the A40. There was no way he felt inclined to help them, and as Jacko, equally confused, peered out at the unfamiliar place names on the signpost where they'd halted, he acted swiftly, wrenching at the door handle and scrambling out on to the grass verge.

Jacko swore and launched himself across the back seat. He was unable to risk a shot, as there were houses nearby. Neal reached back into the car, dashed the gun from Manning's grasp and yanked him out by the throat.

He heard Sylvie mutter a curse as she vacated the driver's seat. Hauling Jacko upright, Neal clouted him on the jaw, knocking him back against the car. He stooped to retrieve the gun, which had fallen to the floor. That was his mistake.

A blast of perfume announced that she was behind him, and as he came up, gun in hand, she hit him from behind. He never knew what she used, but the blow was enough to send him to his knees and drop the gun.

He felt himself blacking out and fought against it furiously; tried to get up but couldn't make it. He was conscious of hands grabbing him roughly and bundling him head- first back into the car. Manning was swearing volubly, and Sylvie berating him in a shrill, angry voice. Then the Citroen was moving off again, and he still inside it with them, although in worse shape than a few minutes previously.

Neal must have lost consciousness for a while because, unusually, the image of his father swam across his mind. Lionel, never one to plead, seemed to be pleading with him. Neal was unable to understand what he was saying. His father was mouthing words, and they were inaudible. *Roger –* was he asking about Roger? In the hiatus of the last twenty-four hours, Neal had had no time to think about his brother. Surely, it couldn't be true that Roger was involved somewhere in all this? And yet that fleeting image – there and gone so quickly – of proud Lionel Gallian imploring him to do – what? It convinced Neal that there was something, some hidden truth, still to be discovered.

A plea, then, for justice? That Lionel, so entrenched in his views, inconsolable in his misery, knew now that he'd been wrong and was urging his surviving son to do all he could to set it right? His addled mind travelled back to Valleronde, the crypt, the church, sitting with Father Julien: the lighting of the candle and the heartfelt, unspoken prayers…

Slowly, he drifted back to consciousness to find himself slumped awkwardly on the back seat with his hands tied in front of him. Sylvie sat before him, driving frantically through the night, head and shoulders bent over the steering wheel; and Manning alongside him, one hand clutching the gun, the other massaging his aching jaw.

Neal rested, his eyes closed, awaiting the return of his senses, coaxing himself into alertness for the next opportunity. He knew they must be close to Braxbury by now. A movement beside him suggested that Manning was checking up on him, and he groaned, shuffled down farther in his seat, head lolling groggily.

Within minutes, they were cruising down Braxbury High Street and swinging into the driveway of The Leylands. Neal stirred himself to wakefulness. The back of his head still hurt, where Sylvie had whacked him, but the pain helped him to focus. The car drew to a halt.

"Wakey, wakey," Manning snarled and dug him sharply in the ribs. He winced, realised Manning had got out; but before he could stir himself to action, Jacko had reappeared, yanking open Neal's door to drag him out by the arm.

"Thought you'd be made of sterner stuff," he grumbled, as Neal blundered out to stand unsteadily beside him. "Must be getting windy in your old age." Even so, Neal noticed that Manning kept the gun trained on him from a discreet distance.

Jacko prompted him to lead the way and, as he stumbled towards the front door of the house, he noticed a second car in the driveway: a gleaming maroon Peugeot 403, with French number plates.

Sylvie was at his shoulder, back to her mocking best. "I think we'll let you ring the doorbell, Neal," she breathed intimately in his ear. "You'll get a nice surprise."

He lurched forward and leaned on the bell. He'd seen the car, and if she meant coming face to face with Armand Delacourt, it wouldn't be nice and would hardly rank as a surprise.

Footsteps sounded in the hall. Two people: that was the surprise. But when the door swung back, and Jill Westmacott stood in front of him, surprise turned to shock, and he stared at her speechlessly.

32

Shock gave way to emptiness. His last vestige of hope had gone, spirited away by her sudden appearance.

A brutal shove in the back propelled him forward, and he almost fell into the hallway, while Jill skipped aside to avoid collision with him.

He looked round at her, bewildered. "Jill?" he stammered. "What *is* this?"

She didn't reply, hung her head shamefully. He saw the beginnings of tears in her eyes.

The response to his question was supplied by a smooth, complacent voice, and only then did Neal notice the man standing at Jill's shoulder.

"Ah, M'sieu Gallian. How good of you to call. Such an inquisitive young man. Alas, I feel you'll give us no more trouble."

"He's given us enough, blast him," Manning grumbled, as he and Sylvie came in, closing the door behind them.

Neal was aware of Delacourt switching Jacko a puzzled glance before turning his attention to Sylvie.

"Ah, *chérie,* you are a delight to behold. Just to set eyes upon you is worth the journey here."

The Frenchman moved forward to greet her with the statutory kisses, as ever making a meal of them. Which gave Neal the opportunity to confront Jill.

She stood before him pale and trembling, her tears now staining her cheeks.

"Oh, Neal, I'm *so* sorry. I've made a complete mess of things. This – this man was waiting when I got to the station. He said he was an old friend of Uncle Lam's from the war, that he was employing a top solicitor and would take me to meet him. I – I believed him and went with him. Oh, I've been such a fool!"

"And once in the car, he chloroformed you and brought you here," Sylvie chimed in, having at last eluded Delacourt's cloying grip. "You really shouldn't make a habit of getting into cars with strange men, Jill, my dear."

"It was an easy mistake to make," Neal whispered. He'd seldom felt lower. He'd promised Wilkie he'd look after his young niece, but the opposition had been a step ahead. He couldn't see a way out of this, was prepared to accept it for himself. But he couldn't see how they'd be able to let Jill go now. He felt sad for her, and angry at himself for not having foreseen the danger.

Jill stumbled forward to hug him, then looked startled as she saw that his hands were tied. However, before she could make contact, Delacourt dragged her away, not too gently, steered her through to the lounge and plumped her down on an upright wooden chair, before slavishly returning to Sylvie in the hallway.

Neal followed slowly, knowing that Manning and the gun weren't far behind. He positioned himself behind Jill's chair, expecting to be moved away. But Jacko backed over to the sideboard, on which stood a tray of drinks. He poured out half a tumbler of scotch, sipped it and gazed over towards them contemptuously. His face looked more evil than cunning, and his small black eyes glinted cruelly. Neal wished he'd hit him harder.

Armand Delacourt came in with Sylvie. His grey hair was swept back over his skull and gleamed with brilliantine. He wore an expensive cologne and looked sleek in blazer, beige flannels and red cravat. But he wasn't a happy man. Neal had been aware of a whispered conversation in French between Sylvie and the antiques dealer, and from the look on her face, they'd been having words.

Delacourt still wasn't appeased. "You have not told me who this man is, Sylvie," he complained, indicating Manning with a derisory hand. "I thought we had no secrets, you and I?"

"As I have explained, Armand." Sylvie's voice was weary. "John is a friend of mine. I can have friends, can I not?"

"It depends on what you mean by friends," Delacourt sniffed. "Not, I hope, a close friend?"

"That's not for you to dictate."

"You know why I am here, *chérie*." The Frenchman's tone was wheedling. "I am so sad about poor Maurice. He was never the husband I would have chosen for you, but that's in the past. I am here because I felt it my duty to offer you consolation now."

The argument had claimed Manning's attention, and he looked on, seeming vaguely amused. The diversion had not gone unnoticed by Jill. She placed her hands behind her and, through the spars in the chair, began to work on the rope around Neal's wrists.

He was relieved that she was alert to the danger threatening them both and, as the heated exchange progressed, felt his bonds starting to loosen.

Delacourt raged on, now seeming on the verge of tears. "I agreed to help you in this, Sylvie, because I presumed this would only concern you and me. What is *he* doing here? I demand to know. Are you playing me false?"

Despite his perilous position, Neal couldn't suppress a pale grin. Sylvie, playing someone false? *The very idea!* But Delacourt's impending disenchantment offered up a tiny sliver of hope.

Sylvie had recovered her composure, her hand caressing Delacourt's shoulder, soothing the hurt, relishing the trap. She was at her most disarming; also, Neal felt, her most dangerous.

"Dear Armand, I am so sorry for this misunderstanding. Above all, I need you here. You play a most important part in my future plans."

Delacourt was about to simper, lulled by her artfulness, when Manning suddenly burst out laughing.

The Frenchman glared at him, affronted. "I amuse you, *m'sieu*?"

"Oh, not at all, old sport." Manning's tone was genial, veiling his menace. "But Sylvie's right. No way we could do this without you. See, Gallian here's been searching high and low for his brother. You'd know all about what happened, wouldn't you? And Sylvie and me reckoned he might have some questions to put to you."

He glanced over, smirking, at Neal. Neal knew what he meant and paid no attention. He was staring at the antiques dealer, who'd suddenly turned pale; and he knew exactly what Jacko was getting at, exactly where this was going.

"You killed him, didn't you, Delacourt? You killed Roger?"

Jill gasped, her fingers fumbling on the knots. She slowly withdrew her hands, for everyone's attention was on Neal.

Delacourt tried to bluff it out. "Your brother, M'sieu Gallian? The army lieutenant who deserted from his company in Valleronde? Oh, you are mistaken if you think that I –."

"He didn't desert at all," Neal interrupted him, his voice slurred with accusation. "Because, as I've always believed, Roger was no coward. I imagine he'll be found in the tomb of Alain Brissart in the church at Valleronde. In fact, I'm fairly certain that you helped put him there."

33

There could be no question of Delacourt's guilt: his face gave him away, and his eyes took on a hunted look. His mouth worked for words, found none, and he started to back away.

Then a change came over him, face and eyes suddenly hardening, and his hand delved madly into a blazer pocket.

Sylvie was first to see the danger. "John!" she shrilled. "He has a gun!"

Manning was quickly alert. He'd fired by the time Delacourt had the gun halfway out of his pocket. The weapon slid from the Frenchman's grasp and bounced once to land in the middle of the thick-piled carpet. He turned towards Sylvie, clutching his chest, his face convulsed and mouth gobbling for words, his protuberant eyes beseeching. Jill screamed, as he sank to his knees and crumpled at Sylvie's feet.

Sylvie stood still for several moments, gazing down at the body of her old admirer with an expression of mild distaste. She exchanged glances with Manning, gave an almost imperceptible shake of the head. He turned and grinned at Neal; and his face was the embodiment of evil, the eyes like small black stones.

Sylvie was looking alarmed. "John – *no!*" But he'd already carefully deposited his gun on the sideboard behind him and was stooping to pick up Delacourt's weapon.

She stepped across the room, gripped his arm, her voice low and trembling with urgency. "*No!* I beg you -!"

In that moment, Neal knew his plan. It would be interpreted that Delacourt had shot Jill as she'd tried to escape, and that Neal and Delacourt had shot each other. Sylvie, once it dawned upon her that she had no choice, would play the shocked innocent, and Manning would disappear, eventually assume a new identity.

There was no longer any hope to be gained from Sylvie's intervention. Manning gently removed her hand from his arm and, without any show of force, pushed her away to stagger back to where she'd been standing, her eyes huge and horrified.

Neal's thought-process was the work of milliseconds. As Manning took hold of Delacourt's gun and started to straighten up, he reacted. His hands were still tied, although Jill had managed to loosen the bonds.

Grabbing the back of the chair, he flipped it over on to its side. Jill tumbled off with a yelp and rolled over to land behind the sofa.

Neal was moving as Jacko brought up the gun. He balled his bound hands into a double fist and clouted Manning on the side of the head with all the strength he could muster.

As Jacko fell, the gun exploded, the shot punching Neal backwards. He knew he'd been hit, willed himself to stay on his feet, teetered forward and threw himself on to Manning, as he struggled to get up. The gun fell from Manning's grasp and bounced away. Neal flung out a hand towards it, couldn't reach it.

Sylvie, looking on in astonishment, went for the gun, much closer to her than the one Manning had left on the sideboard.

She came a poor second. He'd been aware of Jill scrambling to her feet. Despite the searing pain in his side, he smiled inwardly. He'd been right about Jill's resilience. She beat Sylvie to the gun by a good two yards, levelled it at her, snapped at her to keep back, because she knew how to use it. And he was sure she wasn't bluffing. No more the girl-next-door!

Sylvie backed towards the door, her hands in the air, then, believing she was far enough away, snatched up a vase and, swearing freely in French, hurled it at the girl. Jill ducked nimbly, the vase smashed against the wall behind her, and Sylvie took the opportunity to break away.

By that time, Neal had heard the roar of cars on the drive, sirens shrilling furiously. Within seconds, the door had crashed back, and the room was full of police uniforms.

Beneath him, Jacko Manning stirred, and Neal, feeling his strength waning, lifted his head and smashed it on the floor a few times for good measure. The carpet was thick, but the floor beneath it concrete, and Manning was silenced.

Neal felt the wetness of blood seeping through his shirt, and the pain so severe that he became aware of his senses slipping away.

He heard Sylvie protesting haughtily, as she was escorted back into the room by DCI Pilling. "These people burst into my home and held me at gunpoint! I took the opportunity to escape – why are you taking me back in there?"

Incredibly, he caught a glimpse of Colonel Wilkie, his image blurring as he stood over him. What was he doing there? Hadn't Pilling arrested him?

Jill knelt beside him, with one of the uniforms. He'd handed her something, a towel, Neal guessed, and she was pressing it hard against his wounded side in a desperate attempt to halt the flow of blood.

"Uncle Lam?" Her voice was urgent, tearful. "Will Neal be all right? He – he saved my life. Oh, Neal, my darling, please, *please* just hold on. They've said an ambulance is on its way…"

His last sensation was of her lips against his own, and of Wilkie's words of comfort, slurred and inaudible, as he felt himself slowly drifting away.

*

It was only much later that he learned of Wilkie's discovery. Bill Crannock, while acknowledging his own guilt in the drug-smuggling operation, had spoken up loud and clear on behalf of his old CO, to the extent that Pilling took Wilkie's advice and got North Yorkshire police to ask Colonel Johnnie Vosper that important question. As soon as the answer was telephoned back, Pilling released Wilkie, and they set off for Braxbury and The Leylands with two carloads of uniformed officers, for Wilkie felt certain of Sylvie Vernon's involvement.

An ambulance was quickly on the scene, and Jill accompanied Neal and one of the constables to the Radcliffe Infirmary in Oxford. Sylvie was hauled off to Oxford police station, and Pilling and Wilkie were left with the unconscious Manning, whose skull had been fractured by Neal's frenzied assault.

"Well, Colonel?" Pilling asked him. "I take it your suspicions have proved correct?"

"They certainly did," Wilkie confirmed, as they watched Manning being borne away on a stretcher under police guard, although he'd be going nowhere for a while. "That man is a clever rogue – cleverer than I might have given him credit for. Neal Gallian would only ever have known him as Jacko Manning. But when he was in my company in France, I knew him better as Private Harry Doyle."

34

Harry Doyle came clean; or as clean as he was ever likely to. Sylvie Vernon, as was to be expected, employed an expensive lawyer, and the deal they concocted was that Doyle would absorb most of the blame in return for avoiding the hangman's noose, which both Pilling and Wilkie felt he fully deserved.

At best, he knew he'd end up inside for a very long time. But Harry Doyle was resigned to that. He'd gambled and lost. However, the gamble had been well worth taking.

We were in a bar one night in Valleronde, Bill Crannock, Ted Stoker and me. This French geezer slid in and joined us, Armand Delacourt. I never liked him from the off: he was a slimy devil. He'd heard our CO had picked us to go up to the Chateau Garay and make sure it was safe, that Jerry had properly cleared out, as we'd been led to believe.

Delacourt had this proposition to put to us. He was with the local resistance, and he'd guide us up through the woods out of sight of the chateau. He told us the German commandant had lit off in a hurry to save his skin. The place had been brimful with antiques, art treasures and the like, because old Marichaux had been about as rich as Croesus, and as sure as summer follows spring he wasn't coming back.

Von Rinksdorf hadn't had room in his staff car to take everything with him, and there was a lot of valuable stuff still lying around. Armand and his dad were local antiques dealers, and they had a list as long as your arm of private collectors in the USA. All Armand needed was help to get the stuff away. He'd guarantee us a decent cut. Were we interested?

You bet we were. The war wasn't going to last much longer, and none of us could guarantee there'd be much for us in civvy street, we were hard-up, and a shedload of extra lolly could help set each of us up for a while to come.

Crannock was our sergeant, and he had some pull with the CO. So, we went along to the old man and asked if Delacourt could guide us up there. He knew the lie of the land and could help us avoid any booby traps Jerry might have left behind: mines, snipers and the like.

Well, the colonel gave us his blessing. Only trouble was, he insisted an officer should be in charge.

The officer he had in mind was Lieutenant Roger Gallian. Pity of it was, we all liked him: he was a decent bloke. I wondered if we could square him, 'cos none of us wanted him hurt. Bill reckoned he was too straight for that, but he had a plan to side-track him. He'd concoct a story about a sniper and reckoned the lieutenant would go off looking. See, Gallian hated Jerry like poison, on account of his best mate getting killed in the landings, and he was still really cut up about that.

'Course, ironic, weren't it, as we closed in on the chateau, there *was* a ruddy sniper, and he got me? I was all for carrying on but was losing a lot of blood. Gallian applied a tourniquet and ordered me back to camp to get it properly sorted. Just as well I went, 'cos I passed out the minute I got there.

The next day, Stoker came to see me in hospital and told me the rest. There'd been two snipers up there, and it was reckoned they were a couple of guards, who'd sneaked back to see what pickings old Rinksdorf had left behind. Crannock popped one of 'em, and the other scarpered. Lieutenant Gallian went after him. He was all for bringing him back, 'cos he thought he might have information about Jerry's retreat, so our own boys could get ahead and cut 'em off. Apparently, the CO had been keen on bringing back any prisoners, and Gallian was the blue-eyed boy, so was out to set an example.

Crannock watched him go, pleased he'd got his diversion ready-made, and told Armand to get a move on. His old man was waiting outside the gates with a van, and Armand got him to come up.

But the lieutenant got back sooner than expected. The Jerry had run for his life and outdistanced him. And swipe me, there was Armand and his dad bundling all these antiques and the like into their flippin' van. Gallian marched round and ordered him to stop, and Armand pulled a gun and shot him. I mean, he just pulled out a ruddy gun and popped him without a word of warning. Stoker said him and Crannock were struck dumb, helpless, looking on in horror.

Gallian died on the spot; that one bullet did for him outright. But Delacourt kept a cool head. They stowed the body in the back of the van, along with the stolen treasures, and the Delacourts dumped the whole lot in the church crypt after dark. I should reckon Gallian's body ended up in one of the tombs down there. The Delacourts had some pull with the priest about storing valuables there, so's Jerry wouldn't get them. But I'll lay you a pound to a pinch of snuff old Holy Alphonse never knew about what else they'd left.

Crannock and Stoker reported back to the CO. They had no choice but to say that Lieutenant Gallian had gone after the sniper and hadn't returned. Colonel Wilkie took them and some others up at first light to search for him. They found no trace.

'Course, Delacourt had told Crannock and Stoker that if they wanted their money, they'd have to play ball. He backed Crannock's story to the hilt, and the CO reluctantly reached the conclusion that Gallian had deserted. He'd been very close to the pal he'd lost in the landings, and Wilkie reckoned it must've affected him real bad, 'cos he'd been low for days on end.

Well, I was sorry about Gallian, but there was nothing I could do. Stoker assured me I'd get my cut once the Delacourts had sold the stuff on. But they squeezed me out. I never heard another dickie bird from them.

The company moved on a couple of days later, leaving me behind in the field hospital to give the wound time to heal. I came on later with another company, supposed to meet up with the CO, Crannock and the rest at some God-forsaken town on the Loire. But I never got there.

We ran into an ambush, believing Jerry to be a lot farther down the road. A grenade knocked me for six, and when I came to, I couldn't remember much, my head ached like fury, and I was covered in blood.

A couple of geezers lay dead beside me. One of 'em looked as though he'd taken the full force of a grenade: he had no face to speak of.

I don't know what drove me to do it. I sure as hell wasn't thinking straight, but I swapped over our papers, left mine in his tunic pocket. Goodbye, Harry Doyle.

I tell you I was a wreck, physically and mentally. I was out on my feet, didn't know if it was Easter or Christmas, and it was weeks before it all came back to me how those three miserable bastards had cut me out.

I must have staggered on for miles, 'cos the next I knew, I was laid out in this field, and this young girl was bending over me, and she had the face of an angel. Blimey, I reckoned I'd died and gone to heaven. Only thing against that was that she was yelling fit to bust for her mum and dad to get there quick.

They had this farm in the middle of nowhere, and they took me in and sorted me out, and everything gradually came back to me. By the time I'd properly recovered, the war was over. 'Cept that Sylvie and me had fallen in love, and life looked like it had taken a turn for the better, until her dad discovered us up in the hayloft. He chased me away with a shotgun, and I hid up in the woods. Sylvie found me there, and we finished what we'd started. She stole some money from her parents, gave it to me, and off I went. We were both in tears, never thought we'd see each other again. She wanted to come with me, but I couldn't be having that. Where I was heading was no place for a young girl. So, we said goodbye.

35

    I got back to England by an unconventional route, 'cause I knew some people who could fix me up with a new identity. The poor geezer who'd copped it, whose papers I'd acquired, had been called John Mann. Just a short step to John Manning, Jacko to my mates – or those who became my mates.

    Back in civvy street, I had to start from scratch, 'cos I had nothing, and that meant operating on the windy side of the law. I dabbled in this and that – dabbled a sight too much and ended up doing a stretch. When I came out, I decided to go straight until the right opportunities happened along. I met old Bolsover in a pub up in Brum, a beer and spirits wholesaler and a decent old sort, decent enough to take me on. I'd been on my uppers, and I was so grateful that I worked my socks off for him, repping for him in the Midlands. Then he asked if I'd widen my area a tad, temporary-like, and call in on this shop in Braxbury.

    Well, of course, that's where I met Sylvie again. Swipe me, seventeen years it had been, and she'd developed into a real smasher. They say love never dies – well, too true it hadn't, and she said how she'd never forgotten me and always wondered if she'd ever see me again. Blimey, it blew me away!

    Sylvie told me how she was in this unhappy marriage. Vernon had been keen on her when they'd met at this vineyard where she'd been working. Offered her the moon, and she'd leapt at the chance to get away, particularly as, from the age of about twelve, she'd been pursued by this dirty old devil who was a friend of her parents.

    We started again where we'd left off up in the woods beyond her farmhouse. Life was good, and I didn't reckon it could get much better, but it did when I learned the name of this family friend: Armand Delacourt. I remembered him, and that I owed him. I owed Crannock and Stoker too, but particularly him after the way he shot Lieutenant Gallian in cold blood, one of the few blokes in authority I ever respected.

    I spoke to Sylvie about it, and that set her thinking. Vernon no longer had any feelings for her, and she wanted out. But she didn't want to be penniless, 'cause her mum and dad had nothing to leave her. Vernon did, and if she played up to old Armand enough, he'd make provisions for her in his will. So, could we get our revenge on them all: Crannock, Stoker, Delacourt and Vernon? We worked out that we could.

It was easy enough to track down the first two. Crannock had hit hard times. He liked a flutter, and he'd lost heavily. His old CO had taken pity on him and set him up in business right there in Braxbury. He'd worked hard and was doing all right, and by great good fortune, Stoker, who was at rock bottom – nothing new about that – had sought him out, and Crannock had found him a job in a neighbouring village.

I began with Ted Stoker. Met him at his usual watering-hole and put a proposition to him. I knew there was this copper Gallian, who'd nicked me once - our Lieutenant Gallian had been his brother. Stoker would contact him through me and offer up the truth about what had happened at the Chateau Garay. We'd play him off against Armand Delacourt, who was alive and thriving in Valleronde. One would pay us for the information, the other for us to keep our mouths shut. Either way, or both ways, we were quids in.

Ted liked the idea. He was all set to go for it and got blind drunk on the prospect. But once he'd sobered up, he got spooked by Crannock and wondered if p'raps we ought to include him in the scam? But I didn't want that. For starters, I didn't want to run across Crannock, 'cos he'd recognise me as Harry Doyle, and Doyle was dead and buried out in Normandy and wasn't coming back. Stoker knew who I really was, of course, and never realised what dangerous knowledge that was. Crannock was another matter altogether; but Sylvie and me had found a place for him in our plans.

So, I contacted Neal Gallian. He showed up all right, but then Stoker got the heebie-jeebies. He was like a cat on hot bricks, and Crannock must've caught on that he was up to something. Thankfully, Ted ran away, but we met up as we'd arranged, a bit later, which was when the poor sap fell in the river. He was so drunk he could hardly stand. Pity I can't swim, else I might have been able to save him…

The van that nearly ran me down that night was Vernon's. Sylvie was driving and damn near clipped me. Swipe me, talk about realistic! But it was enough to convince Neal Gallian that I was in fear of my life. He hid me away – blimey, old Flo did me proud! What a cook she is – makes me wish I'd stayed there. And I was able to work unhindered, keeping in touch with Sylvie by public telephone. We staged my abduction – Sylvie in the van again – and in the meantime, she'd bribed Crannock's mate, Phil Slant, to lift the latest consignment from the shop while old Maurice was away. 'Course, Slant was putty in her hands, till I showed up. Things got nasty, and the little bastard came at me, right there in Vernon's shed. He attacked me, and I did for him, though I swear it was self-defence.

I bundled his body in the back of his van and made off from there. It was a stroke of luck, 'cos Slant and me were about the same size, and he was going to do me the favour of passing off as the late Jacko Manning.

See, it was part of our plan to implicate Colonel Wilkie. Not that I had any axe to grind with him; he's a decent old boy. But the summerhouse had to go, 'cos in pride of place on the wall there, Sylvie had noticed once when she'd been taking tea with the colonel, this whacking great photo of him and his company before they set out for Normandy, with Harry Doyle smack bang in the middle of it, grinning like a chimpanzee.

Of course, the colonel had to make himself scarce, else how would he explain away Manning's charred body in the ruins of his summerhouse? He was pally with Crannock too, so it would look as if he had some part in the drug-smuggling op with Bill and Maurice Vernon. According to Sylvie, he visited their wine shop pretty frequently.

I knew Wilkie from way back too, and he was no duffer. Given time to sit and ponder, he might well have worked out what was going on, why the summerhouse had been torched, and by a process of elimination come around to Harry Doyle.

Sylvie reckoned we should track down Wilkie and keep him quiet till we were ready, 'cos he could scupper all our plans. I followed him up to his place in Lincolnshire, but he gave me the slip. I decided to wait for him at the cottage there, but then Neal Gallian showed up, and I was hard put to it to get away. So, in the end I had to be content with putting the cops on Wilkie's trail and fitting him up for the body in the summerhouse.

Sylvie staged the quarrel with Vernon, fired him up so that he dashed off to have it out with Crannock. I was waiting for him at the warehouse and popped him with the colonel's gun before he was able to get off a shot at me. Then I threw down the gun, ran off and, lo and behold! down comes Crannock from the office, kneels gaping at the body and picks up the gun. Couldn't be better.

And finally, Delacourt. He was the big fish for me. It was no problem for Sylvie to entice him over here. She got him to pick up Wilkie's little niece from the station, and my plan was for it to look like Delacourt had topped her, and that him and Gallian had shot each other. That would've finished it off a treat, but Sylvie was dead against it.

Personally, I would have been sorry about the two of them. I couldn't have given tuppence for Delacourt, but it had got to the stage where they knew too much, and something would have had to be done.

But there we go. Wilkie and Gallian did for me in the end. And Crannock, of course, blast him, speaking up for the colonel the way he did. Loyalty, I suppose. Honour.

Blimey, amazing what gets into some people.

36

But Harry Doyle was loyal too; as, in her way, Sylvie Vernon was with him. The expensive lawyer did his job in saving Doyle from the gallows. His pleas were that Stoker had fallen into the river, and the deaths of Phil Slant, Maurice Vernon and Delacourt had arisen out of self-defence. There were no witnesses to the first three, and Sylvie, Jill and Neal all admitted that Delacourt had reached for a gun with intent to kill.

Doyle got life, but he played down Sylvie's part in the whole business, along with her stunning performance in the witness box, testifying that she'd been brutally maltreated by both Vernon and Delacourt. However, she didn't walk away and was probably one of Holloway Prison's most glamorous inmates for a number of years.

DCI Pilling, along with Neal and Wilkie, wasn't happy about it, as they were unanimous that she'd been the brains behind the operation. Neal wondered if Sylvie would stick around for Harry Doyle, if and when he came up for parole.

Somehow, he doubted it.

*

But the trial didn't happen for several weeks, as both Neal and Doyle were in hospital for nearly all of those.

Neal awoke that first morning, knowing exactly where he was and why he was there. He'd been lucky: it had been a flesh wound, although he'd lost a lot of blood. So, he'd ended up again in the Radcliffe Infirmary, having been at the wrong end of a gun, more or less in the course of duty.

However, he didn't feel low. It was rather as if he'd come full circle, as if he'd been given a second chance. The ghosts – the face in the warehouse, Clyde, Helen – had receded into the shadows. They'd haunted him for far too long.

That time before, when he'd first awoken, they'd been there, within and all around him, nudging him forward into a grey and meaningless future. Now, he felt absolved; more so after the vivid dream he'd experienced before awaking.

He'd dreamt of his father: Lionel in no mood Neal had ever witnessed before, relaxed and smiling. And when had he ever known his father smile, unless grimly and cynically? He couldn't call it a vision, for it had been nothing more than a dream. But he took it as a sign that his father, after years of self-inflicted shame, was finally absolved and whole again.

When Wilkie came to visit him, Neal had learned that the colonel had undertaken to see Roger's case re-opened. On the new evidence, he was confident that the ruling of the court martial would be overturned, and Roger posthumously acquitted.

As Neal had suspected and Harry Doyle's confession brought to light, Roger's remains were discovered in the church crypt at Valleronde, in the tomb of the heroic Comte, Alain Brissart. In time, Neal was glad to be able to give his dear brother a Christian burial.

Wilkie went on to explain that Bill Crannock had come to his rescue, absolving him of any part of what had gone before. DCI Pilling had followed up the colonel's plea to get in touch with Johnnie Vosper. In the hours he'd spent on the run, Wilkie had had plenty of time to reflect. And he'd wondered about Harry Doyle. Might there be a loophole there? He begged Pilling at least to ask Vosper the question: could he supply the name of any soldier who'd gone missing after the ambush at Pont du Garde in August 1944? The answer had come back: Private John Mann. Buoyed by the similarity of the name to that of Jacko Manning, Wilkie had urged Pilling to act swiftly.

So, convinced now that Wilkie had put them on the right track, Pilling allowed him to tag along. When they'd found Briar Hedge unoccupied, the next port of call was The Leylands, in time to whisk Jill to safety and Neal to hospital.

Pilling came to see Neal too. He urged him to rest up, make a full recovery and give serious thought to re-joining the force. Neal promised to do that, particularly as the DCI wanted him in CID rather than back in uniform.

Finally, there was Jill. The flowers, the fruit, the magazines, the get-well card in his side ward, the presence at his bedside that he'd sensed rather than seen on those occasions when he'd stirred: the movement around him, none of which he could any longer attribute to any ghost. All that had been Jill.

Above and beyond everything, her slight figure filled his vision. He wanted her in his life, because she was someone he could believe in; someone who believed in him.

"She's spent hours here, moping around, worrying about you," Wilkie confided. "You saved her life, and I tell you she won't forget that in a hurry. I've been trying to get her to come home for something to eat, but I might as well save my breath."

And that next time he'd dozed, awaking with a start. The colonel had dropped in and was about to leave. He was over by the door, and Neal's eyes snapped open to see Jill walking towards it, walking away from him, as Helen had gone that time, and he'd never seen her again.

He called out desperately, "Jill! *Please* – don't go!"

Wilkie had gone with a smile and a wave, but Jill had turned, come back to him, her face bright with love and her eyes sparkling, as she sat down beside him and clasped his hand in both of hers.

"I don't intend to," she whispered reassuringly. "Ever."

*

The Scars of Shame, copyright Michael Limmer 2024

MYSTERY THRILLERS
from MICHAEL LIMMER

Michael Limmer is the author of seven mystery thrillers, of which *The Scars of Shame* is the latest. He's also a short story writer of both mystery and Christian fiction and all profits and royalties from the sales of his work are shared between three Christian charities. Mike's most recent novels, *Marla*, *Past Deceiving* and the novella *Time Knows No Pity* are all available from Amazon in paperback and e-book formats.

If you've enjoyed this book, please visit Mike's website at
mikesmysteries.co.uk

*

Neal Gallian will return in

The Relentless Shadow

A link between two cold cases from the past…
Will it help Neal Gallian find a murderer in the present?

For more information on this and other novels featuring Neal Gallian, please visit Mike's website as listed above.

Printed in Great Britain
by Amazon